M000295117

Played Out

The Making the Play Series

L.M. Reid

SCARLET LANTERN
Publishing

Scarlet Lantern Publishing

Prologue

Billy

Never say never.
  "You're never going to play again."
"I can fix this."
"It can't be fixed."
"I'll do whatever it takes."
"There's nothing to do—you're done playing football."
"No. No. No."
I shoot straight up in bed, my body covered in a cold sweat from the nightmare. Only, it isn't a nightmare. It's my reality. One that haunts me even in my sleep.

Scrubbing my hand over my face, I attempt to clear the visions that keep hitting me like a runaway train despite the fact that I'm awake. The football field, my knee twisted in a direction it shouldn't be, my doctor's voice telling me I'm irreparable.

Heart pounding, blood boiling. I'm not only terrified, but I'm also furious. Everything I worked for, everything that matters to me —it's gone.

Done.

Over.

Finished.

For years, I listened to my grandmother repeat the old adage "never say never." It was my slogan, my catch phrase, what I lived by.

Until I no longer could.

Never again will I play football.

Never again will I be on the field.

Never again will I be able to live out my dream.

Suddenly, the word never takes on a whole new meaning for me.

I get out of the bed and pad over to the dresser where the nearly empty bottle of whiskey sits. I grab the bottle by its neck and drink the remains of it.

From the moment the doctor said the words, everything inside me shut down. The man I once was isn't the man I am today. That guy, he wouldn't be clutching this bottle in desperation, eager to chase the dream away. And he sure as hell wouldn't be heading to the kitchen for more of the amber liquid to dull the pain.

My hand pulls the knob and opens the cabinet, my eyes searching for the bottle—my vice. Where it should be sitting is empty. Nothing but a Post-it note stuck to the shelf.

Knock the shit off, it reads.

Mason. Fucking asshole.

I rack my brain, trying to figure out how in the hell he managed to sneak it out of here last night. Or for that matter, why? I'm not his fucking kid. I'm not his fucking problem. Why the hell is he sticking his nose into shit that's not his to worry about?

The quick answer is that he's Mason Ford and he does whatever the fuck he wants.

The empty bottle still in my hand, I throw it across the room in anger, not even cringing when it shatters all over the kitchen floor. I'm too angry, too desperate.

I need that drink more than I need my next breath. Without it, I don't really give a damn about breathing anymore. My life is empty. My heart, too.

Jesus Christ, I've already lost everyone I love. Did I really have to lose football, too?

My hand grabs the set of keys I tossed on the counter, then I step into my shoes and head out the door. The engine revs and I pull out of the parking space, intent on getting that bottle of whiskey. Music blaring, I speed down the street. The nearest liquor store is only a few blocks away, but I'm in a hurry to drown out the pain.

The rearview mirror illuminates with red and blue flashing lights. "Fuck."

I try to remain cool as I pull the car to the side of the road. Just another discrepancy between the old me and the man I've become. Until tonight, I've never even so much as been pulled over. And now, I'm on the verge of arrest.

"License and registration." The officer's tone is harsh, anger-filled. Even though I know he can not only see my face but recognizes it, I can also see that he doesn't fucking care.

I hand him the documents. He barely looks at them before asking, "Have you been drinking?"

His tone is authoritative and unforgiving. "Uh... I had a few last night." Honesty is always the best policy, even if it's only partial honesty. "I know I was speeding, but—"

"Speeding?" The officer shakes his head. "You were doing more than speeding. You were all over the road. I'm going to need you to step out of the vehicle."

"Yes, sir." I open the door and step out of the car like he asks.

The straight line he tells me to walk certainly doesn't look straight to me. And I sure as hell am incapable of walking it.

"Sorry, Officer, let me try again. I, uh... I just woke up." It's a pathetic attempt at trying to hide my lack of sobriety. Pathetic enough that the officer sees right through it.

"I've seen enough," the officer tells me. And based on the tone in his voice, it's not in a good way. "I'm going to have to take you in."

I nod, my head hung. Just when I thought things couldn't get worse, I go and make a fucking mistake like this. All these years of trying to be a good guy, to do the right thing—all down the drain in one fucked-up moment.

Sitting in the jail cell, waiting for my one phone call to show up, all I can think about is what I've turned into. I hate the unrecognizable man who stares back at me in the mirror every day. I don't want to be him, but I feel so lost and out of control that I don't know how to be the real me anymore.

Months of rehabbing my knee to be told the degenerative condition can't be treated or reversed. Hearing that one bad hit could render me incapacitated was more than I could bear. Do I give up the career I love? Or risk never walking again to continue it?

The answer was a no-brainer—I had to give up football. Still, knowing that didn't make it any easier.

"Well, well, well." Mason's voice echoes through the holding area as he steps in front of the cell I'm being held in.

"About time," I say, making my way toward him.

He raises an eyebrow at me. "You called me in the middle of me making love to my wife. Sorry if I wasn't in a hurry to bail your ass out of jail."

After all the shit Mason's pulled over the years, he's going to give me shit about one mistake?

"Fuck you. Just get me out of here," I demand.

"Quite the demand from the guy behind the bars." He steps closer to the cell, his glare holding mine. "What the fuck were you thinking?"

I slam my hands against the metal bars. "I was thinking some asshole took my bottle of whiskey and I needed more. Maybe if you had minded your own fucking business, this wouldn't have happened."

"Maybe," he begins, "if you quit feeling sorry for yourself and—"

"Enough." Avery's voice breaks through our argument. "This isn't the time or place."

She's followed into the room by an officer who unlocks the cell door and slides it open. When I step through, I come face-to-face with Mason. "Go to hell."

When I finally emerge from the police station, Mason and Avery are waiting by their rental car.

"I'll find my own way home," I tell him.

"Billy, stop," Avery tells me. "We just want to help."

"You may want to help." I point at Mason. "He just wants to watch me suffer."

"You know damn well that's not true," Mason says. I can tell by looking at him that he's holding back from coming at me. "But you need to quit doing this shit."

I shrug. "Why? What else do I have to do?"

"Jesus Christ, are you kidding me?" Mason shouts, throwing his hands into the air. "Coach, report, start a business. Do something. Because this little downward spiral you're on? It's only going to get worse and rock bottom is not a place you want to be."

"I'm already there," I shout back. The anger subsides, the sadness and misery taking over. "I'm already there."

Chapter 1

Sadie

"Get back here, you little stinker," I call out to Bryce as I chase him across the yard, water balloon in hand.

He got me first. And I fully intend to pay him back.

His sandy brown hair bounces as he runs. It's gotten a little shaggier these last few days and I just haven't had the time to cut it.

I throw the balloon at him, a near miss as it lands next to his feet. He laughs, loud and long, and the sound is like music to my ears.

It feels like forever since I've heard him laugh like that and I am willing to do just about anything to keep him doing it. Even if that means throwing him a football-themed party for his eighth birthday in a few weeks.

Bryce hasn't really been a huge fan of sports; his interests have always leaned more toward cars and Legos. But that all changed the moment his dad left. Not only is Jon a sportscaster, but he is a football fanatic. With his father gone, Bryce became one, too. I can't help but think that this whole football obsession is his way of trying to reach out to his dad. Something he hopes will bring his dad back, if only for the birthday party.

I don't have the heart to tell him that it won't happen. That his father is nothing but a selfish prick and is off "doing him" with some twenty-one-year-old on his arm. All of which is fine by me. Bryce and I, we are doing just fine on our own. Without him.

Still, as I chase Bryce through the yard, another water balloon aimed at him, my heart breaks for him. This wasn't how it was supposed to be. We were supposed to be a family. He was supposed to have two parents who love him. Not one who loves himself more than anything and one who only loves himself.

Lost in thought, I feel the cold liquid on my skin before I even realize what happened.

"Got you." Bryce laughs as he does a happy dance in the middle of the yard.

"Payback," I shout at him.

Before I can throw the balloon, a familiar car pulls up in front of the house next door to us. The gorgeous blonde steps out of the car, her phone to her ear as she chats a million miles a minute. Never missing a beat, she continues her conversation as she yanks the "For Sale" sign out of the ground and carries it under her arm back to her car.

A few moments later, she drops all pretenses and runs in her heels toward Bryce, scooping him up in her arms.

"Put me down, Aunt Jules," he says, his voice still filled with happiness and amusement.

"Not until... your mom hits you with that water balloon," Jules says, setting him down just in time for me to break the balloon on his head.

"Aw, man," Bryce yells.

"Told you I would get you," I say. Nearly out of breath and soaking wet, I stop and smile at Jules. "So, it's really sold, huh?"

Jules nods her meticulous head. "Yep. Paid cash. Gave me way too much commission. Best deal ever."

"And you're still not going to tell us who bought it, are you?" I pry.

"Not a chance in hell."

"Aunt Jules said a bad word," Bryce interjects, ratting my best friend out as though I didn't hear the word myself.

I stick out my hand for her dollar, the one that will be put into the swear jar Bryce made for her.

God love my college friend, but the woman has the mouth of a trucker.

Jules sticks her tongue out at Bryce as she sets the dollar in my hand. "Just wait until you get older. Don't expect me to help you out when you get in trouble."

"What's the big secret anyway?" I ask, changing the subject.

"It's not a secret, not really. It's not like he asked to remain anonymous. It's just—"

"It's a guy," I yell to Bryce, who has since moved on to the swing set. Though, it doesn't surprise me considering the amount of work it's going to take to get that place habitable. The house has amazing potential, but years of no one caring for it have left it in desperate need of some TLC.

"Maybe he can teach me sports," Bryce says.

"I can teach you sports," I reply, earning me laughter from both Bryce and Jules.

"Honey, you were a cheerleader, not an athlete," Jules says. "Besides, I've seen you throw a ball."

"Whatever," I say, waving her off with my hand. "Are you staying for dinner?"

"Nah, I have to run. Have to head into Remington to finish up the paperwork with your new neighbor."

Remington? Why in the world would she have to go into the city to finish this deal? "Ah, the plot thickens."

"You'll find out soon enough."

"Soon enough? As in when?"

"Tomorrow." With a wave, Jules is off.

"Did she say anything else?" Bryce asks as he runs up to me.

"Not a clue, little man." I ruffle my hand in his hair. "What should we do for dinner tonight?"

"Let's go to the diner. I have a taste for pancakes."

Breakfast for dinner, our favorite.

"Sounds like a plan," I tell him. I remain quiet for a moment. "Know what else?"

"What?"

I smash another balloon on his head.

"That," I shout as I run into the backyard.

With it being such a beautiful day, we decide to walk our water drenched selves over to the diner. By the time we make it there, we're mostly dry.

When Bryce slides into the booth across from me, I can't help but marvel at what a little man he's becoming. He looks so big sitting there with his menu open, pondering what he's going to choose.

"Hey, you two. Long time no see. What can I get ya?" Sally asks as she stands at the edge of the table with the pen and pad in her hand. No iPad, no technology, just good old pen and paper.

When I first came to New Hope, I just wanted to escape. I needed someplace safe for Bryce and me to go. Since Jon was busy doing his own thing, he wasn't really concerned with us leaving. He made promises of visiting, but I knew he wouldn't. Especially not when he landed the gig with ESPN. It was a national spot, and it wasn't long before he began traveling with the teams.

So, while Jon was out living it up, Bryce and I settled in with Grams and made a new life for ourselves here in New Hope. Any worry I had about the transition for Bryce died in the water the day we moved in. A little boy down the street, Tommy, came over and introduced himself, and they've practically been inseparable ever since. What had started out as a temporary situation quickly turned into a new life for us. A new start. And with Jules here, it just made it all the easier.

I'm eternally grateful to my grandmother for allowing Bryce and me to move in. Even more so for her letting me buy her house. I'm still not entirely sure if moving into the retirement community is what she wanted, but she swore to me it was. Otherwise, I would have never taken her up on her offer. She seems happy. And she seems even happier to watch Bryce and me building a life for ourselves.

"What do you think he'll be like?" Bryce asks, disrupting my thoughts.

"Who?"

"Our new neighbor."

Tapping my finger against my chin, I think about his question. My luck, he'll probably be a jerk. "Hopefully he's nice."

"And fun."

One can hope.

"Jules said he's moving in tomorrow. We should stop at the store and get him a little something to welcome him to the neighborhood."

"I have a better idea."

Of course he does.

"You should make him a batch of your chocolate chip cookies."

I nod in agreement. "I like that idea. You want to help me?"

He nods eagerly as Sally sets our plates in front of us.

"Better eat up. We have work to do," I tell him as he begins to dig in.

Chapter 2

Billy

"Billy? Is that you?" an all too familiar voice asks.

I hang my head, my gaze dropping to the empty glass in front of me. I can't face the man standing next to me. I don't want to. A month has passed since I've seen him. A lot of things have changed since then. Though, with the empty whiskey glass in front of me, I'm afraid he'll never believe they have. I can only imagine what he's thinking—what he thinks of me.

"It's not what it looks like," I tell him, my gaze still focused on the glass rather than his face.

"Well, that's a relief," he says, taking a seat next to me. "Didn't feel like bailing you out of jail a second time."

"Lesson learned. I assure you."

"Is it?"

I glance over at him, his eyes on the glass, his eyebrow up in question.

Last month, I hit rock bottom. Or at least I hope that was rock bottom because if it wasn't, I would hate to see what comes next. I'm certainly not fully recovered, but I'm on my way. If I want to keep it that way, I need to get out of Wisconsin.

"It's water."

"If you say so."

I slide the glass across the bar top. "See for yourself."

Mason stares at me for a moment before sticking his nose in the glass. I hate that he does it, but I don't blame him. When we last saw each other, there would have been a good chance that I was drinking. And that I was drunk. Satisfied that I'm not lying to him, he smiles.

"I haven't had a drop since that night. I swear."

"Well, I have to admit, you do look better than when I last saw you. Not that you ever really looked good to begin with."

The comment, chastising as it is, makes me smile. It brings a sense of normalcy that I've been lacking. "You're such an asshole."

"And yet you're the one who wanted to be my friend."

"We all have regrets," I chide.

"How's the knee?"

"Fine."

Albeit a vague answer, for all intents and purposes, my knee is just that—fine. I can walk. I can move. Sure, I hit the occasional snag with it if I overdo it, but for the most part it's good. However, it's not rated for football, which means regardless of how "fine" it is, I still can't play. One false move. One bad hit. That's all it would take to land me in a wheelchair. As much as I hate not playing, I'm fairly certain that not walking ever again would be more of a hardship.

So, I did the smart thing. The right thing. I quit. I walked away from the only thing I ever truly loved. Besides my mom and grandmother. While I know it's the right decision, it sure as shit is not an easy one to swallow. In fact, I've been choking on it since I made it. At first, I had hope. I busted my ass trying to rehab my knee in hopes that the doctors were wrong, that I could make some miraculous recovery. I was wrong.

That's when the finality of my football career really set in. From then on out it was a downward spiral. Until the arrest. The one that not only made my life a living hell in the tabloids but simultaneously saved it. Had it not been for that night? I don't know where in the hell I would be right now. Certainly not sober. And definitely not the new owner of a house in New Hope.

"What are you doing back in Remington? Why didn't you call?"

"Is that a serious question?" I ask with a laugh.

After the arrest, the tabloids had a field day with me. Even though I quit drinking, every eye in town was on me. I couldn't go to the store without people trying to catch a glimpse at what was in my cart. If they weren't doing that, they were looking at me with pity. Oh, how the mighty had fallen. Once the golden boy of the team, that one mistake stole that from me. Everything I had ever done was under scrutiny to determine if I was actually a decent guy or not.

"I don't know, man, I just couldn't take it back in Wisconsin. The looks, the tabloids, it was all too much," I admit. "And I didn't call because, frankly, we didn't end things on the best of terms last time I saw you."

Mason nods in understanding. He's been through the same shit, though, at the time, his was well warranted. While I deserve what's coming to me for making such an asinine mistake, I don't know that I deserve the lengths the press is going to. Especially that dick Jon Hart. After all I did for him, the fucker turned the tables on me and used me to advance his fucking sportscasting career.

Mason shrugs. "You were in a bad place. That doesn't change the fact that we're friends."

I nod, guilt settling over me. "I guess I just didn't have the balls to make the call."

"Okay, well, let's leave that shit in the past. Where are you staying? Avery will be thrilled you're back."

I shake my head. "My stay in Remington is nothing more than a blip on the radar. A stop on my way back home."

"You're going to New Hope?"

I nod.

"Why?"

"I just need some peace and quiet. Some time to clear my head and get my shit straight. There's no way in hell I'm going to be able to do that in Wisconsin. Or even here for that matter."

"And you think you're going to get it there with all those small-town gossips running around?" Mason emits a soft chuckle, clearly remembering the many stories I told him about growing up in New Hope.

"I don't know, man. When I sat down and tried to figure out what came next, all I could think about was New Hope, my grandmother's house. So, I figured, why not? What else do I have to do?"

The small town that I dreaded growing up in, a place that was more boring than watching paint dry, is the only place I can even fathom going right now.

"So, then why are you here and not there?" Mason asks.

"I had some... business to take care of."

"Oh, really?"

Without even seeing his face, I can picture it. I know exactly what he's thinking and where he thinks this is leading. A woman.

"Not what you're thinking."

"So that woman walking this way isn't with you?"

I glance to my left, to the busty blonde headed in my direction. She's with me all right. Just not in the way Mason is thinking.

"Mason, this is Jules. My realtor," I tell him when she approaches.

"Nice to meet you... Jules," Mason says, his voice laced with insinuation.

"What's he doing? Why is he looking at me like that?" Jules asks as she stares at Mason with wide eyes.

"He thinks we're sleeping together," I tell her.

Her laughter fills the quiet bar. "As if." She takes a seat next to me. "I do have a friend, though."

"No."

"But—"

"No."

"What about you?" she says, turning the question to Mason, who in turn holds up his left hand and shows off his wedding band.

"Your losses." Jules returns her attention to her phone and whatever business deal she's working on now. As if she needs another one after the way she extorted me.

"What do you need a real estate agent for?" Mason asks.

"I bought a house." The notion brings a smile to my face. It's about the only thing that has these past few months.

After my grandmother died, I sold her house to the first bidder, which just so happened to be a leasing company. I hated to do it, but I had no time to take care of or deal with it then. I was at the height of my football career and trying to maintain a house thousands of miles away didn't make sense. Now, I have nothing but time and all I could think of was to go back home and buy that house. Lucky for me, money talks and the new owners walked. Though, from what Jules has said, years of renters have left the place in less than livable conditions. More than once she tried to sell me on something bigger, better, and brighter. Something that would be fitting of a man of my caliber. Her words, not mine.

Sure, I can afford it. I can afford anything I want, but none of it sounded appealing. I wanted to go home. Really go home. And Grandma Ruth's was the only real home I ever knew.

Jules tried to dissuade me and showed me pictures of the place. The exterior seemed to be in decent repair, but the interior was a whole other story. Nothing had been updated, much of the wallpaper and fixtures things that I grew up with. Not to mention the garbage and clutter left behind by unworthy tenants.

"You bought a shithole," Jules chimes in despite her not being a part of the conversation.

"Watch it," I scold her. "That's my grandmother's house. Besides, nothing a little elbow grease can't fix."

Mason quirks an eyebrow at me.

"What?"

"Is this some sort of thing where you can't fix your leg so you're going to try and fix this house instead?"

"That's exactly what it is," Jules replies.

"Butt out," I tell her, giving her a quick scowl before turning back to Mason. "So, what if it is? Is it that terrible of an idea? Doing something to keep my mind off of things? Controlling something when I can't control shit else in my life? I'm fucking miserable, Mase. Have been for months. I need something. I need a purpose. I need to figure out who the hell I am going to be now..." I choke down a sob. "Now that I can't be who I wanted to be."

"You're a great man. A great friend. Isn't that enough?"

"You know as well as I do that lately I haven't even been that. I need this, Mase."

"On the plus side, at least we'll be close. Avery can help you continue some therapy. We can come visit."

I nod in agreement. Her PT program is honestly the only thing that helped me make it along this far. I was beyond grateful to her when she flew out to Wisconsin to help me start the program and work with the team therapist. A stringent program, lots of time, and at least I can walk without pain. Mostly. And it's all thanks to her and the surgeon who managed to perform miracles.

Mason holds up his beer in a toast. "Well then, congratulations, my friend."

I lift my recently refilled water glass and clink it against his bottle. "Cheers."

Chapter 3

Billy

"So, you and Travis still a thing?" I ask Jules as I make my way down the road.

"Oh, God, no. That ended years ago." She shakes her head violently as she speaks. "We were—"

"Prom king and queen," I recall.

"And a whole big mess underneath it all. We're better off the way we are."

"And what way is that?" I pry.

"Living in the same town, avoiding each other like the plague?"

I nod, not fully understanding, but knowing that based on the look in her eyes, I need to leave well enough alone.

Lucky for me, she's all too happy to change the subject. "So, that friend I told you about..."

"The one I already told you I'm not interested in?"

"Yes, I know. You've made that more than clear. While I think you'll regret those words, that's not what I was going to say. I just thought I would let you know that she's your neighbor."

"My neighbor? You were trying to set me up with Loretta?"

Loretta Riggins. She's a feisty woman in her mid-seventies who not only owns the local bar in New Hope but was also my grandmother's neighbor and best friend.

"Oh, please," Jules says with a laugh. "You couldn't handle Loretta. No, Loretta moved out and her granddaughter, my bestie, moved in."

The idea of Loretta not living in that house never even occurred to me. Part of me was looking forward to the familiarity. The crass comments, the home-cooked meals. All things that at one time I wanted to run from, I find calling to me now. Simplicity. Peace. A sense of family.

"I can't believe she moved."

"That's the part you're focusing on? Not that your neighbor is smoking hot?" Jules shakes her head in disbelief. "Yes, Loretta moved. New Hope is really starting to blow up. They built a small maintenance free community and Loretta jumped at the chance to move. Especially since Sadie needed a place to stay. Poor girl."

I can tell by the way she says it that she wants me to pry, to ask about this woman I have zero interest in pursuing anything with. Based on her "poor girl" phrase, I don't know why in the hell she would even consider me an option for her friend, knowing the shit I've been dealing with.

"Sounds like she's been through enough. She doesn't deserve to have to put up with my shit, too."

"You're right, she has been. But maybe you two could help each other—heal."

"Help each other?" I ask, giving her a curious glance.

"Help. Hump. Whichever." Jules has a wicked gleam in her eye.

"Jesus, Jules," I choke out, nearly spitting the sip of coffee I had just taken onto the dashboard. "You're even more trouble than I remember."

"Me? I'm not the one with the DWI."

I cringe at the sound of the word. "Not my proudest moment."

"Clearly. Doesn't sound much like the nice, straitlaced guy I went to school with. Where's he at? What happened to him?"

"He got kicked in the ass, so I sent him packing."

"I get it and I'm not trying to be a bitch here. I just hate seeing you like this. You used to be—"

"I used to be a lot of things. Including a football player. The moment he left, so did the nice guy. That okay with you?"

Jules doesn't say anything. She just continues to stare out the window at the familiar road before her.

"Shit, Jules, I'm sorry."

"There he is," she says with a hint of a smile forming.

"I'm just having a hard time dealing with all of this," I tell her, the admission nearly fucking killing me.

"We all go through rough times. What matters is how we come out on the other side of it. And I predict, you'll be fine. It's just going to take some time."

"Always the cheerleader." I laugh, which causes her to go into a random cheer I recall hearing from the sidelines of the football games back in high school. "So, what else has changed that I should know about?"

My last visit to New Hope was for my grandmother's funeral. I was just starting out in the pros, so I didn't have much time. I flew in for the wake and flew out immediately after the funeral. And between those two events, I didn't venture outside of her house much. I was lost in grief and memories.

I still have a hard time wrapping my head around the fact that she's gone. Five years. Where in the hell has the time gone?

"Oh, you know. A new coffee shop, some new stores. Nothing major. I promise, it's the same boring town that you remember."

A satisfied sigh escapes me. Just the words I needed to hear.

As we make our way through the town, I realize how right she is. So much of it is the same, but so much is different. Including the brunette who now occupies the house next to my grandmother's.

As Jules pulls into the drive, I slide my glasses off and take in a better view of the woman who is going to be my new neighbor. My head tilts to the side as I watch her bend over to pick a flower out of the flower bed in the front of the house.

"Told ya," Jules says, her voice startling me out of the fantasy that was beginning to form in my head.

"Shit, you scared me." I turn to face her.

There's a pleased smile on her face as she gets out of the car with me following suit. "That woman you just weren't looking at is the very woman you told me you wouldn't be interested in."

I roll my eyes at her. "I'm not interested. I was just—"

"Checking her out?"

That's one way of putting it. I resist the urge to adjust myself, my dick twinging in delight from just a glance at the woman. Even though I know Jules has her eyes on me, I can't seem to tear mine away from my new neighbor.

"Does she have a name?"

"She does. But you'll have to find that out for yourself." Jules grabs a bag out of the back seat. "Come on, let's go check out your new home."

Staring at the house for a moment, memories of my childhood come flooding back. Good memories. The ones I cling to at night when the football demons try to attack. The longer I look at it, the more reality sets in. The house is in deplorable condition. Christ, what have I done?

"Like I said, shithole." Jules makes a move toward the house.

Shaking my head, I grab the other bag and sling it over my shoulder, all the while regretting my decision to buy the place back sight unseen.

"Come on," Jules urges. "Let's see what kind of mess is inside."

Only, the word mess seems to be the biggest understatement I've ever heard. The place is trashed, deserving so much worse of a term than the word shithole that Jules keeps using.

"Are you sure you don't want to stay at a hotel until you get things fixed up?" She picks up and tosses—something—to the side. "Or fumigated?"

I look around, completely disgusted by what I'm looking at. A wave of guilt comes over me. This is all my fault. I did this. I sold the only place I ever called home without a second thought to some money hungry rental company. All because I was too busy to be bothered with it.

You reap what you sow, right? And me discarding this place like I did? Well, payback's a bitch and I'm definitely getting what I deserve.

"I'll be fine."

"Suit yourself," she says as she tosses me the keys. "I'm getting out of here before something eats me."

Scrubbing my hand over my face, I try to focus and make a game plan. But the longer I stare, the deeper I dig, the more I have no clue where to even start.

What the hell did I get myself into?

Chapter 4

Sadie

"Who is it, Mom?" Bryce asks, trying to push me away from the window so he can get a better look.

"I don't know," I tell him as I peer over his head.

Small-town, nosy gossip. It's something Bryce and I adapted to quickly. We stare out the window, trying to decipher who is moving into the home next door to us. The one that had been empty for months after a long line of renters, each worse than the last, but was recently purchased by some mystery man.

A man.

That is all the information I got out of Jules, the local real estate agent and my best friend.

"Why wouldn't Aunt Jules tell you who it is?" Bryce asks.

It's a good question. One I don't have an answer to. At least not one I can tell him. Telling my seven-year-old son "Because your aunt Jules is a bitch" probably wouldn't be the mom appropriate answer. But that's exactly what she's being right now, withholding information from me. Especially since she's never done it before.

Why is she hiding my new neighbor's identity?

Who is the mystery man?

"You two look pathetic," Jules says.

The sound of her voice makes both Bryce and me jump. "You scared us to death. Where in the world did you come from?"

"The back entrance. Figured you creepers would be stalking your new neighbor."

I sneer at her before peering out the window again.

"He's already inside. And he was checking you out."

Why the thought of some man ogling me sends a tingle down my spine, I have no idea. I should be appalled. Instead...

"He was?" The surprise in my voice is more than evident to Jules, who shakes her head at me.

"I don't get it. I don't get why you don't see how fricken hot you are."

As much as I appreciate her compliments and the fact she can utter them sincerely, I don't see the same thing she does. It might have to do with my husband leaving me for a more attractive, younger woman. Or maybe it's the stretch marks and scar from the cesarean I had when I had Bryce.

Whatever the reason, I just don't see the hot girl. I see a mom. A mom who hasn't had sex in over a year, which is probably why I'm having tingles just from the idea of some man checking me out. A man who, with my luck, is some old grandfather. Or worse, a drug dealer.

"Are you going to tell us who 'he' is or not?" I ask, even more curious now knowing that he was looking at me.

"See for yourself." She nods her chin toward the window.

A moving truck pulls into the driveway at the same time that a man steps out of the house. Tall, broad chest, dark hair, and an amazing ass.

The way Jules has been hiding the identity, I would have thought it would have been someone I knew. Nothing about the man is familiar. Hot, but not familiar.

Bryce is next to me, and I can see his mouth fall open the minute he lays eyes on the man. I'm not sure what or how he recognizes him, but he does. Excitement bubbles over in him, and he jumps and shouts.

"Someone want to clue me in?" I say, utterly confused.

"It's Billy Saint," Bryce shouts. The information does nothing to help me.

"He's a football player," Jules replies. "Well, an ex-football player."

"Yeah, he got hurt at the end of the season and they said he can't play anymore," Bryce informs me. "Can I go meet him?"

He begins to run to the door, but my mom sense has me reaching for his shoulder and grabbing on. "Not so fast. Let the poor guy get settled in."

I'm still not sure how he plans on doing that considering the place is a wreck. Which begs the question, what the hell did he buy it for? Football player or ex-football player, the guy has to have money. The fancy SUV parked in front of the house is evidence enough of that. So why buy some rundown house in a small town?

"He grew up here," Jules says, as though she can read my mind. "In that house. His grandmother owned it."

"He's Ruth's grandson?" I ask.

"Yep."

I continue to stare at him through the window, taking in every glorious inch of his taut body. When he glances toward the house— my house—I startle and jump back, nearly knocking Jules over.

Her laughter flows through the house. "If you weren't such a creeper, you wouldn't have to jump like that."

"Do you know him?" I ask her. "Aside from the whole realtor thing, I mean?"

Her arm drapes over my shoulder. "As a matter of fact, I do know him. And aside from being a fine piece of ass, he's also a really nice guy."

It doesn't take a genius to figure out what it is that she's insinuating. "Not interested."

"Girl, you need to get interested. In someone. Preferably him. Or else"—she lowers her voice—"your lady parts are going to dry up and fall off."

"Pretty sure that's not how that works."

"Maybe not, but damn close. You need to live again, Sadie. You need to enjoy life."

Glancing over at Bryce, I smile. "I enjoy plenty."

Jules's smile is soft as she glances at Bryce and then at me. "You need to enjoy things outside of Bryce. Things for yourself."

A part of me knows she's right. Bryce already has one parent who's doing that, though. He doesn't need another. As much as I would love to sow some wild oats, enjoy some me time—Bryce is top priority. He's my reason. My sole purpose in life.

"I'm not saying you have to marry the guy," she continues on. "But a night here, or a night there, rolling around in his bed." She finishes with a shrug.

I scoff at the idea. "Even if I wanted to, there is no way in hell that some rich, hot football player is going to want to... you know... with a mom who has stretch marks and scars."

"And great boobs, a killer ass. Quit selling yourself short, Sadie. You're hot. You're smart. You're a total catch. And considering he was checking you out when we got here, I'm pretty sure he wants to... you know... with you."

Hard as it is, I tear myself away from the window and the man who has me intrigued. "Are you going to hang out for a while, or do you have a client?"

"Why? Want me to introduce you to Mr. Stud?"

"We made cookies for him," Bryce shouts.

"Cookies, huh? Your mom's famous cookies?"

Bryce nods enthusiastically.

"It was Bryce's idea," I say defensively before she can try to make a big deal out of nothing. Hell, it's not like I even knew what the guy looked like yesterday when I made them.

"Maybe we should take them over to him," Bryce suggests.

"Yes, yes, you should." Jules is all smiles as she encourages my son.

"He probably—"

"Would love some cookies while he watches the movers bring stuff into the house."

Only it isn't just the movers doing the moving. Even at my distance, I can see the ripple of muscle in the man's arm as he carries a table with what looks like minimal effort.

Bryce and Jules just stare at me. "Fine, let's go," I say, grabbing the tray of cookies as I head to the front door. They are both hot on my heels.

"Hey, Billy," Jules shouts out. His head whips around at the sound of her voice. "Your neighbors can't wait to meet you."

Maybe he can't hear it, but I sure as hell do. The insinuation and seduction in her voice.

"I'm going to kill you," I whisper to her. The threat earns me nothing more than a laugh from her.

Bryce takes off running and comes to a halt right at Billy's feet. He's talking a mile a minute. "I'm Bryce and that's my mom and you know Aunt Jules and I'm so excited to meet you. You are such a great football player. Or you were. Sorry about that. But it's super cool you're going to be our neighbor now and—"

"Bryce, breathe," I say.

The hulking football player doesn't seem to mind, though. He stands there, smiling down at Bryce. "Nice to meet you, Bryce."

His eyes fly up to meet mine. "And you are...?"

The blue of his eyes is a contrast to the black of his hair. And the look in them floors me. I attempt to speak, to complete our introductions, but nothing comes out. The man has literally taken my breath, and my words, away. I clear my throat, trying to regain my composure. "I'm Sadie Hart."

He extends his hand in my direction. "Nice to meet you, Sadie Hart."

Juggling the tray of cookies in my hands, I free one in order to shake his. The moment his hand touches mine, a jolt soars through me. I yank my hand back, nearly dumping the tray of cookies as I do so. Lucky for me, those football player reflexes manage to catch them and steady me all at once.

"You okay?" he asks.

I nod. That's it. I don't speak. I don't do anything. I just nod. Like an idiot.

"These for me?" Billy asks, still holding the container of cookies.

"Yep. Mom and I made them for you." Thank God for Bryce and his endless enthusiasm. He's saving me from literally dying of embarrassment in front of a man I'm going to be seeing day in and day out. "They're the best. Everyone loves her cookies."

"I bet they do. I would invite you in, but Jules was right, the place is a shit—" He stops himself. "Sorry. I meant that it's a mess."

"It's okay. Aunt Jules swears worse than that," Bryce says with a laugh. "We have a swear jar at home. Have to put a dollar in every time you say a bad word."

"Oh, yeah? Well, since I almost said one, I should probably pay up." Bill pulls some money out of his pocket and hands it to Bryce.

Bryce's eyes widen at the twenty-dollar bill. "Do you plan on swearing a lot?"

"Just to be safe," Billy tells him.

"You don't—" I begin, but Billy holds up his hand to stop me. "It's fine, really. And with the way this place is looking, I'll probably have to give him another one sooner rather than later."

"It looks like you have a lot of work ahead of you."

"You don't know the half of it."

Resting my hands on Bryce's shoulders, I give them a squeeze. "Why don't we let Mr. Saint get settled?"

"Maybe I can come by tomorrow and—" I place my hand over Bryce's mouth.

"Leave Mr. Saint alone," I tell him.

"It's Billy. And Bryce is welcome anytime." He ruffles Bryce's hair, much the same way I do. "It was nice to meet you. Both of you."

His eyes lock with mine and I stutter out a final greeting, "W-welcome to town."

I walk away in a hurry, dragging Bryce behind me.

"What did I tell you?" Jules whispers. "The guy is hot for you."

Based on how damn soaked my panties are from touching his hand, seems like I might be hot for him, too.

Chapter 5

Billy

S tanding in the middle of the room, I take in everything around me. The outdated and torn wallpaper. The destroyed floors. The slight pest problem. Clearly, the renters who had been allowed in here didn't care for the place. Still, as bad as the place is, I'm glad I bought it. Despite all the damage, it still feels like home.

It also kind of feels like a metaphor. I'm the house, damaged and in need of repair. Only, I'm irreparable. The house, however, is not. And I'm the only one who can fix it. That alone gives me a sense of purpose. Finally, after months of feeling like I was drifting in a sea of nothingness, I feel like I'm on the right path. Hell, I might even feel happy. I know I'll feel even better once I get this place back to where it should be.

The question is: where in the hell do I start?

And when it's done, what the hell do I do with it?

I'd barely given much thought to the repairs, but now that I'm here, I can't help but wonder what comes after them. Is this it for me? Is this my future? Or is it just a steppingstone in my healing process?

I have opportunities out there, just like Mason said I would. Even with my now tarnished record, I've been offered both coaching and reporting jobs. But is that what I want? Would I be able to handle being around football that much without ever being able to play again?

The answer to that question right now, without a doubt, is no. It's hard enough when I scroll through the TV and catch the highlights. My chest aches every time. I have no idea if that will ever go away.

Grabbing my cup of coffee, I make my way onto the rickety back porch and sit down on the steps. Soaking in the morning sun, a strong cup of coffee in my hand, I try to stop myself from continuing down this rabbit hole that I know can only lead to bad things. That's not what I'm here for.

"Hi." I hear a small voice off in the distance. Looking around, I see a little boy with sandy brown hair. He's standing at the edge of the yard, just on the other side of the fence.

"Hey there, Bryce," I say.

He looks ecstatic that I remembered his name. "Hey."

Ecstatic or not, he still seems a little nervous. Considering what I probably look like at the moment, I don't know that I would be rushing over here either. I'm sure the exhaustion is showing on my face, not to mention the displeasure I still feel from not being able to drink them away.

That's not to say I want to drink. I don't. I just hate that there's nothing there to dull the pain. Something. Anything. At the moment, the face of the little boy seems to be helping, though.

"You want to come over?"

He nods and steps through the gate. He fumbles with the latch but can't get it closed. "Guess I'll have to fix that, too."

"You can fix things?" he asks as he walks toward me.

Kid has no idea what a loaded question he just asked.

"I'm going to try."

A moment later, he's standing in front of me, his eyes focused down on the ground. "Sorry you got hurt."

"Me, too," I admit. "It really su—stinks."

"You look like you can walk okay, though. My mom and I were watching you out the window yesterday."

Him and his mom? The thought of Sadie watching me, checking me out the way I had her, gets me a little more excited than it should. Especially since, from what Jules said, Sadie Hart has seen her own fair share of bad luck. No need to drag her into mine.

"Yep, I can walk okay. Running on the field and getting tackled wouldn't be good for my knee, though."

He nods as if he understands when he couldn't possibly. Hell, even I don't. No matter how many times the doctor said it, no matter how many ways he explained it, I still can't grasp the condition I'm in. One false move is all it would take to require a full knee replacement. Or worse.

"Why did you come to New Hope?"

I nod back toward the house. "I grew up here." There's a mortified look on his face that makes me chuckle. "It didn't look like this when I lived here. In fact, it was... perfect." I only wish I had realized that back then. Then maybe the place wouldn't look like this now.

"My great-grandma used to live in that house," he says, pointing to Loretta's house. "But she let my mom buy it and moved to some old people's place."

"What about your dad? Does he live in New Hope, too?" His face falls at the mention of his dad. Shit. Well, now I know the shit that Sadie's been through. "You don't—"

"He left."

Smooth move, Saint. "Shit, kid. I'm sorry. I didn't mean to upset you."

Bryce stands a little taller, wiping the emotion from his face as though him doing so is going to somehow impress me. "I'm not upset. And now you've used two dollars in the swear jar."

"That I have." I chuckle. "Hey, uh, you want to come in and see some of my football stuff?"

The sullen look on his face disappears and is replaced with a beaming smile. I sigh, relieved to see him happy again.

"Wow, you're tall," he tells me as I stand up.

"Eat your veggies and you will be too one day."

We make our way into the house, and I lead him to where I have a box of some football memorabilia.

"This is so cool," Bryce says as he holds the football from the Super Bowl last year.

It is a neat idea thinking about who has touched that ball. As a kid, I would have died for an opportunity like this. The look on Bryce's face mirrors what mine would have looked like had I ever been in his shoes. His happiness makes me feel better than I have in months.

"My dad left, too," I admit to him. Not because I want to press him on the issue, but because I want him to know that I get it. Reaching into another box, I pull out a hat and set it on top of his head. It's a little big but looks cute as hell on him.

"Wow." The complete awe in his voice makes me smile.

"As soon as I find a marker, I'll sign it for you."

"Really? Tommy is going to be so jealous."

I can't help but chuckle. I had a Tommy of my own back in the day. Someone I loved to hang out with but would have done anything to make jealous as hell, too.

I hear panicked shouting from outside, followed by banging on my front door. I pull open the door and Sadie is standing before me wearing nothing but a short pair of shorts, a tank top sans bra, and a panicked look in her eyes.

"Have you seen my son? Bryce? We stopped by yesterday and—" Her voice is filled with sheer terror.

"Relax, he's fine," I tell her. "He's in the other room."

The shouting stops, her shoulders slump, and she storms past me into my home and toward the direction I'm pointing.

"Hey, Mom, check out all this cool stuff," Bryce says when she walks into the room.

"You scared the crap out of me. You can't just take off like that. I had no idea where you were." Bryce is frozen to the spot as his mom explains the fear his disappearance instilled in her.

"It was my fault," I say, feeling guilty and not wanting the poor kid to be in trouble.

She turns her attention toward me. "Damn right it is. I don't know who you think you are or why in the hell you would think it's okay to let a little boy you don't even know into your home, but it's not."

"I didn't think about it like that. I was just trying to be nice," I say. "I'm sorry. I didn't mean to—"

"I'm sure," she says as she grabs Bryce's hand and helps him to his feet, then leading him to the door.

"I really am sorry," I say, following them out.

She directs Bryce to go home.

"Bye, Billy," he says with a wave as he walks across the yard.

"Stay away from Bryce," his mother tells me, bringing my attention back to her and the hazel eyes that are both glaring at me and turning me on.

"It was a bad move, I'll give you that, but that's no reason to ban me from the kid. We live next door to each other."

"My kid, my rules." She makes her way down the steps and onto the sidewalk.

Looks like any chance I had of playing nice with the neighbor just went right out the window. Good thing I already decided she was off-limits as anything but my neighbor because I'm fairly certain I just blew any chance of making nice with her. Still, I find myself watching her the entire way back to her house, my brain unable to see the fire in her eyes. A fire so bright, so deep that despite the anger it resulted from, was sexy as hell.

Chapter 6

Sadie

B ryce stares at me as I continue to yell at him for leaving the house without permission, for talking to a stranger, then going into said stranger's house. And I keep on yelling because of the million other awful things that ran through my head when I couldn't find him this morning.

"I'm sorry, Mom."

"Sorry doesn't cut it, Bryce." Angry, scared, powerless. Those five minutes were the most awful moments of my life.

"Billy was—"

"I don't care what Billy was doing. Or saying. I don't want you going over there, and I don't want you talking to him anymore."

"But, Mom, he still needs to sign my hat," Bryce whines.

Only now, ten minutes after I dragged him out of our new neighbor's house, do I notice the hat sitting on top of his head.

"We're giving that back," I inform him.

"But, Mom—" Bryce whines.

"No buts, mister. Just... go to your room."

Bryce stalks off, stomping up the stairs, each step louder and heavier than the last, until finally the door to his room slams shut. The sound rattles me momentarily but gives me an opportunity to fall onto the couch with a heavy sigh, the fear of not being able to find him exiting my body. Bryce had never done something like that before, never so much as stepped foot outside of the house without at least telling me where he was going.

I was so grateful he was safe and sound right next door. Until I saw the look on his face. The adoration in his eyes for a man he barely knows. There was a light in them that's been missing since his dad left. And hope. Hope that wasn't going to be fulfilled. That right there only solidifies my decision. I need to keep Bryce away from Billy. Not only because he's a stranger, but because having him around will only put ideas in Bryce's head. Like getting attached to a man who is more than likely going to leave town. I won't let him get hurt again. Not by his father and sure as hell not by Billy Saint.

Instantly, I became angry. Who exactly I'm angry with is still unclear, but the only person I could take it out on was the man standing in front of me. The man who let my son into his home and made him smile like that. The man who, like his father, is undoubtedly going to fail him.

There's a knock at the door and for a moment I contemplate even getting up to answer it. Then I remember Grams is coming over for lunch and she loves to be early. I shake the residual anger off and plaster a smile on my face as I pull the door open.

"Hey," the deep, sexy voice says.

My smile fades, but that doesn't mean my heart beats any less. In fact, it quickens its pace at the sight of him. "What do you want?"

Billy holds up the tray I had given him yesterday with the cookies on it. "Those were the best cookies I've ever eaten."

"Great," I say, allowing the anger to seep back in. I reach for the tray, but he yanks it away from me.

"I also wanted to apologize. Honestly, I didn't mean anything by it. Especially not to scare you. I messed up and asked him about his dad…"

"Why would you do that?" I nearly shout the words, becoming more furious with the man.

"I, uh…" A small, sheepish smile settles on his chiseled face. "I was just curious."

"Yeah, well, don't be. The last thing Bryce needs—"

"It wasn't Bryce I was curious about when I asked."

"Oh my God, that's even worse," I tell him. "The poor kid idolizes you and you were what, trying to hit on his mom?"

Billy's face falls. "No. I, uh… Shit. This isn't going the way I planned."

"Then why don't you do all of us a favor and just leave. Leave my house, leave us alone. Hell, leave town. I don't care. I just don't want any part of whatever it is you're trying to do."

"I'm not trying to do anything. I just wanted to be nice. I wanted to let him know he isn't the only one with a dad who left. I wanted to make him feel better."

I walk back to the couch where Bryce left the hat. When I return to the door, I shove the hat into Billy's chest. "Don't."

With my other hand, I slam the door shut and rest against it. Billy's words, "I wanted to make him feel better" repeat in my mind. I appreciate the sentiment, but I also know what bonding with Billy in any way will do to Bryce. And if he's being honest, if he truly knows what it's like to have a dad who left, he would know that.

A moment later, there's a knock at the door. I turn and yank it open. "What?"

"Is that any way to greet your grandmother?" Grams asks with a confused smile on her face.

"Sorry, I thought you were—" Her face becomes etched in concern. "No, Grams. I thought you were my new neighbor."

"Not quite the way to greet a neighbor either," Grams says as she steps into the house.

"When he's infuriating as hell, it is."

Grams follows me into the kitchen. "Pretty hot, too."

"I hadn't noticed."

Her laughter fills the room. "Bull. No way not to notice that man. Been a few years since I've seen him, but I can't imagine he looks any worse for the wear even with that knee injury."

"Can we talk about something else, please?"

"Did you introduce Bryce? I bet he would get a kick out of a real-life football player living next door."

"Oh, they met."

"Brycie must have been over the moon."

"Yeah, especially when creepy neighbor lured him into the house." I pull out the items I need to begin to make our Sunday brunch. "I've told Bryce not to talk to him anymore."

"Lured him?" Grams laughs.

"Yes, lured him. He told Bryce he had football stuff in his house to show him."

"He does."

"It's weird. And I don't want Bryce around him. Besides, it will only cause him more heartache when Mr. Football God decides to up and leave. He's suffered enough."

"The man barely moved in. What makes you think he's going to be leaving anytime soon?"

Slamming the bread on the counter, I turn to my grandmother. "It doesn't matter if it's tomorrow or two years from now. No way is he sticking around New Hope. And no way am I letting Bryce become attached to another man who's just going to break his heart."

"His? Or yours?"

"That doesn't even make sense. I'm not attracted to him, let alone in love with him. And what I do know, I don't like." Except for the way he looks. It's impossible not to like that.

"Billy is—"

"Hey, Grams," Bryce says as he bounds into the kitchen.

"I thought I told you to go to your room?" I lift my eyebrow as I ask the question.

"I did. But I heard Grams and knew she would be mad if I didn't come down and give her a hug and kiss."

Bryce plants a kiss to Gram's cheek, her arms wrapping around him as he does. Then they both turn to look at me, smiles on their faces. I've been had. And they both know it. "Fine. You can be out of your room while Grams is here. The minute she leaves—"

"I know, I know. Back upstairs."

I shake my head and turn back to cooking. The sounds of the two of them chatting, much like Grams and I did when I was a kid, make me smile. And just for a moment, I forget I'm angry. I forget how much I hate everything Bryce has had to go through. And, most importantly, I forget how happy he looked when he was with Billy. Because if I don't forget that, I might not be able to keep my word.

Chapter 7

Billy

Stepping into Loretta's was like stepping into the past. While much of the downtown had changed and upgraded, Loretta's stayed the same.

Every Sunday, my grandmother and I would join Loretta and Cliff at the bar. The two of them would sit at the bar, gossip about whatever happened in town that week, while Cliff and I played pool and darts until my heart was content. Or until Grandma and Loretta stopped talking. Whichever came first.

I take in the surroundings, grateful to see the interior really hasn't changed that much. Sure, she had done some upgrades, but for the most part it still had that down home feel.

"Well, well, well, if it isn't Billy Saint." Loretta's voice booms through the bar. "Honored to have a man of your caliber stepping foot into my little old bar." The moment I hear the voice, I hang my head. The sarcasm dripping from it is thick as molasses.

"I missed you too, Loretta," I say as I look up at her with a smile.

It's still pretty early and there isn't much of a crowd yet, thank God. I'm not exactly ready to deal with the whole town questioning me and sticking their noses into my life. I know it's going to happen, just not today. Not after having to deal with my sexy, single-mom neighbor. The one who currently hates me and is part of the reason I came here today.

"You look good," I say as I lean over the bar and press a kiss to her cheek.

"Such a flirt," Loretta says with a wink. "What can I get ya?"

"Just a water," I reply. She eyes me curiously. As much as I would love a drink right now, something strong enough to drown everything out, it's for the best that I don't. Me and alcohol seem to be on a slippery slope. No way do I want to end up on the wrong side of the bottle again. "And maybe one of your famous burgers."

Back when I was a kid, Loretta ran the bar, and her husband, Cliff, ran the kitchen. Still, it was Loretta's recipes that made the bar and the food famous.

"Coming up," Loretta says as she sets a bottled water in front of me.

She returns a while later with the burger. "So, what brings you back after all these years?"

"Oh, you know, a bad knee, career ending injury... depression."

"Depression?" Loretta says, her hand waving the notion off. "A guy like you got nothing to be depressed about."

"Football was my life," I reply. "It's a little shitty knowing I'll never play again."

Understatement of the year.

"True. But that's not all that you are, Billy. Not who you are."

"Then who the hell am I?"

Because for so long, that's exactly how I identified myself. The football player. Especially after Mom and Grandma were gone. I'm not a son. Or a grandson. I'm just Billy, the football player.

Or, at least, I was.

"I can't tell you that," Loretta says as she rests her hand on mine. "But I know there's more to you than a football. And I'm sure you'll figure it out in your own time."

I may not agree with it, but I appreciate the sentiment nonetheless. "Thanks, Loretta."

She nods, then slaps my hand. "Now, what did you do to go and piss my granddaughter off?"

I smile, surprised it took her this long to bring up. "Honestly, I'm not quite sure."

I know what I did, letting Bryce into my home without her permission, was wrong, though I don't think it warrants the deep-seated hatred vibe I'm getting from her. Hell, the woman slammed the door in my face. I've never had that happen to me before. Mason, sure. Other guys, yes. But not me. I'm not that guy.

"That's because she isn't either." Loretta laughs. "Sadie's been through a lot these past couple years. Her marriage falling apart, her husband leaving her for a younger woman. Not to mention him leaving Bryce." Loretta shakes her head. "That's been the hardest part. He's basically left Bryce and never looked back. Nothing more than an occasional phone call or card over the past year." She pauses for a moment. "Sound familiar?"

I nod, those feelings from when my dad left flooding me. "That's just it. I asked Bryce about his dad and when he said he left, I felt like shit. I know how he feels. I know what it does when someone brings it up. And..."

"You just wanted to make it better?"

I nod again.

"There's a little bakery three doors down. Sadie loves their chocolate croissants." She holds up her hands. "I'm just saying."

"Thanks, Loretta. How's the new house?"

A huge smile spreads across her face as she tells me about the new senior community she's living in.

When I'm done with my early dinner, I head out of Loretta's and make a pit stop at the bakery she told me about before heading home.

"What do you want?" Sadie asks when she pulls the door open.

"Peace offering," I say, extending the dessert Loretta told me was her favorite.

"How...?"

"Your grandmother." I scrub my free hand over my chin. "Listen, we got off on the wrong foot. And considering that not only are we neighbors, but you're also Loretta's granddaughter, I would like to fix that."

"Did she put you up to this?"

"Who? Loretta? No. I just..." Christ, what in the hell is wrong with this woman? And why do I fucking care so much? "I'm sorry about what happened with Bryce. I didn't mean anything by it. I should have checked with you."

"Yes, you should have."

"I know that now and I promise you, nothing like that will ever happen again. Maybe we can start over. You and Bryce could come for dinner. We could get to know each other. He could have some fun looking through all my old football stuff. What do you say?"

"I say, thank you for the croissants, but I'm not interested in having dinner with you. Or anything else for that matter. Please, just leave us alone."

Chapter 8

Sadie

Staring at Jules, I wait impatiently for her to agree with me and be outraged at Billy's behavior. It doesn't come, though. Instead, she laughs.

"What is so funny?" I demand.

"Okay, it was wrong of him to let Bryce into his home, but he did apologize." She picks up the box with the chocolate croissants that I've refused to eat. "A few times. Besides, I just don't get how you can be angry with a man who looks like that."

"You don't have kids. You don't understand."

"Maybe not, but what I do know is that Billy is a good guy. He would never let anything happen to Bryce."

"You can't be sure."

"And you can't keep everyone at arm's length because you don't want Bryce to get hurt."

My head whips in her direction, her words taking me completely off guard. "I can and I will. Bryce has suffered enough. Any pain I can spare him, I will."

"I don't disagree. But, Sadie, you can't protect him from every hurt."

"I can damn well try," I argue, tears stinging my eyes. "I failed him with his father. I won't let something like that happen to him again."

Jules's hard candy-coated shell begins to melt as she wraps her arms around me. "Oh, honey. You didn't fail him. Jon did."

"I just can't bear to see him get hurt again, Jules."

"What about you, though? What happened to the girl who lived in the moment? The one who enjoyed the hell out of life?"

"She got married and had a kid. And then she got divorced and has to do it all on her own. She doesn't have time for 'fun.' Besides, didn't we just go over this? I enjoy plenty. I enjoy..." My gaze drifts to the window. More specifically, to the man outside of it mowing the lawn. Shirtless. Tanned skin. Muscles.

"Watching the man you hate cut the grass?"

"Thank you for staying," I tell her as I grab my bag. "I'll be home as soon as I can."

Jules shrugs. "And I'll be passed out on the couch when you get here. Have fun at work."

As I head to my car, I make sure to keep my head down and my eyes off the sexy man next door. It's not until I slide into the driver's seat that I allow myself a look. A decision I regret because when I look up at him, he's already looking at me. And waving. Without returning the acknowledgment, I speed down the driveway and in the opposite direction of where I need to go. All in the name of not having to face him.

"Hey, girl," Holly says as I step into the pediatric unit at the hospital where we both work.

I love being a nurse, so taking a job at a nearby hospital was a no-brainer. As much as I love it here, I have to admit I prefer to work in the private sector. My previous job in Dr. Lamont's office had been the perfect match. I was able to be home with Bryce much more often and I had been able to create deeper connections with my patients. Unfortunately, working at a doctor's office in New Hope or anywhere nearby, short of Remington, isn't going to pay what I need it to. And despite the fact that Gram's sold her house to me for well below market value, I need the money. I'm a single mom of a very quickly growing boy. It won't be long before he's eating me out of house and home.

"Hey, Hol. How's it going today?"

We go through a rundown of our patients. A couple of our kids have been released. Others have joined us. And worst of all, one of our repeat customers is back. Poor Jack. This kid has spent practically his whole life fighting and now he's having to do it again. The brain tumor that just won't go away.

When we finally finish charting and making our first set of rounds, I collapse into the chair.

"Have you seen him?" Holly asks as she jumps up and sits on the desk right next to my chair.

"Seen who?" I ask, confused.

"Billy Saint," she says with a roll of her eyes, as though I was supposed to know what she was talking about from her ominous question. "I heard he moved to New Hope."

How had she heard that when I hadn't even known until I laid eyes on him? Hell, my best friend sold him the house and she wouldn't even drip a word of it to me. Not that I would have known, or cared, who he was. I still don't.

"Yeah, I guess," I say in an attempt to blow the conversation off.

"He is so hot. I would happily help him nurse his knee back to health," she gushes. "Or anything else he wants."

"His knee is already healed. He just can't play."

"And how do you know that?"

The light in room 208 flicks on. "Duty calls."

Not that call or any of the others throughout the night deterred her from prying. After what felt like the hundredth time, I finally broke. "Because he's my neighbor, okay?"

Her eyes widen, her smile broad. She looks like a little kid on Christmas morning. "You lucky bitch."

"I wouldn't go that far," I tell her. "The guy is a jackass."

"Still, he's hot."

"Looks aren't everything."

"No, but they help. And from what I've heard, he's a really great guy. Like runs a kids' charity and volunteers for several organizations. He's amazing."

"Let's just agree to disagree."

"Oh my God, did he dump you?"

"What?" I exclaim, wondering where in the hell she would have even come to that conclusion from. "No."

"Why else would you possibly hate him?"

"I have my reasons," I tell her.

"Miss Sadie, Miss Holly," Jack's small voice says from the other side of the desk.

Rushing to his side, I put my arm around him. He's visibly weakened from his treatment earlier today. "Hey, bud."

"I don't feel so good," he says as he rests his head on my shoulder.

I lift him into my arms and carry him back to bed while Holly gets the anti-nausea medicine we know he needs.

"I just want to feel better," he says softly as the medicine kicks in, and he drifts off to sleep.

I smooth his hair with my hand. God, how I want that for him, too.

Chapter 9

Billy

I'm on the field. Running, hitting, falling. Blinding pain. I glance down at my leg, the position it's in—unnatural. The silence in the stadium deafening as I lie there, unable to move. The looks on the faces of those surrounding me are bleak. Each of their voices repeating, "He's never going to play again."

I argue through the pain. "I can. I will."

Laughter. Louder and louder. Not only the coaches, the doctors, but the fans, too. Everyone is laughing. No one understands the pain.

"I have to do this. I have to get better."

The words "You're done" fill the air.

Then she appears.

Sadie.

The scowl on her face, the anger in her eyes.

"I'm sorry."

"Just leave us alone."

"I can't."

More laughter. Her laughter. "No one wants you, Billy. You're done. You're no one."

I jolt up in the bed, sweating and panicked. Stupid fucking dream.

Throwing the covers off me, I get out of bed and head to the bathroom. I turn the faucet on, the water I intended to splash onto my face spraying me in it and soaking the entire room.

"Son of a bitch," I shout to the empty room, my fist hitting the sink.

The pain coursing through my fist is nothing compared to what I felt when I injured my knee. But I'll be damned if the idea of Sadie laughing at me, telling me that she doesn't want me doesn't feel a hell of a lot worse.

After cleaning the sopping mess in the bathroom, I lie down in bed. My eyes remain wide-open despite my attempts to shut them. Unwilling to relive that nightmare, regardless of how stupid it seems now, I don't sleep. Instead, I stare at the ceiling and think. Not about the injury, or my inability to play anymore. No, I think about Sadie. I think about why she doesn't like me. Most of all, I think about what I can do to fix that.

Why in the hell do I want to fix that?

Getting involved with anyone in any capacity right now is a bad idea. Getting involved with a single mom who's been through hell and back? The worst idea.

I shift uncomfortably in my seat, the rock-solid appendage in my pants becoming even more uncomfortable. That, right there, is why I want to fix it. Until I laid eyes on neighbor girl, the damn thing had basically been dormant since my injury. One look at her and all that changed. And despite the fact I've jacked off three times thinking about her already, it's still ready and raring to go.

Sick fuck.

That's what I am for thinking of her like that.

I shove off the uncomfortable couch, both horny and frustrated with myself.

Last night, I had thought that ripping up the carpet would be therapeutic, especially after my run-in with Sadie. Something to free the extra adrenaline she has coursing through me. The nightmare I suffered through proof that wasn't the case. Standing here now, I hope that sanding the floors will be more helpful. Restoring what's broken and giving it new life.

Not having done this before, it's a crapshoot as to how it will go. But isn't that my life lately? Isn't that what this entire project is? Just one big crap shoot while I'm trying to figure out what to do next and hoping like hell that I don't fuck it up?

At least the floors I can afford to fix.

I turn on the floor sander, ready to blast the hell out of these floors, only the sander is way more powerful than I expect it to be. Gripping the handles tighter, I hold on for dear life. Years of vigorous training and muscle building go right out the window as the machine drags me clear across the room. I hold in the scream that threatens the moment the sander takes off.

Finally, with a more ready and powerful grip, I manage to take control, leaving the deeply sanded streak in my wake. As I continue on, I gain more control. Something that I've been lacking recently despite my grueling physical therapy to recover. Football, my degenerate knee issue, all of it is out of my control. But now, here in this moment, I am in control.

Even if it is only of this damn floor sander.

Still, it feels good. Great even. Control. Precision. Determination. The feeling settles over me and is exactly what I had been searching for and more than I hoped for all at the same time. Stripping the floors, watching the old, damaged material disappear and the fresh clean slate appear, I feel a sense of accomplishment. Purpose. And it feels damn good.

Out of nowhere, I feel a soft hand on my arm. A touch that not only startles me but ignites me. I release the sander and watch as it continues forward and bashes into the wall. My eyes fall to the hand that's still on my arm, then up to the face it belongs to. Sadie. The shocked look on her face is covered by the hand that's not touching me. A touch I don't want to walk away from but have to before the equipment makes a hole in the floor.

My hand yanks the cord out of the wall and the sound and motion of the sander come to a halt. I stand there, waiting for the apology she owes me. Not only for scaring the hell out of me, but for barging into my home—uninvited.

Fat chance of that happening.

"Do you have any idea what time it is?" she yells, her voice loud enough to hear clear across town.

"Six?" I reply with a shrug.

After that nightmare, there was no turning back. Between thoughts of her and my defunct career, sleep wasn't an option anymore. Normally, I would get a workout in, but there's no way the gym in this town is open at this hour. If it even has one. Last time I was here, the only thing close to a gym was some yoga studio on the downtown strip.

"Exactly. Six. In the morning. Do you not sleep? Because I do. And this town has noise ordinances, and you broke them."

As sexy as she is, as much as I want her right now, I just want her gone. For the first time in what feels like forever, I felt alive. I felt like I had control. And she took that away from me.

"What are you going to do? Call the police?"

It was a joke. Well, it was supposed to be. The fact that red and blue flashing lights now shine through my window tells me that what I find amusing, she clearly doesn't.

"You have got to be kidding me," I say. There's a satisfied look on her face. "Do you seriously have nothing better to do?"

"What I need to do is sleep and you ruined that."

There's a knock on the screen door before the officer enters. My lips curl into a smile when I lay eyes on him.

"Got a call about someone disturbing the peace," Travis says. Travis Barnes, aka my Tommy.

Sadie points her finger in my direction. "It's him."

Travis looks me up and down, then turns to my new neighbor. "He sure looks like someone who would be disturbing the peace. What do you want me to do with him, Sadie?"

"Fine him. Or arrest him. I don't care. I just want him to be quiet." Sadie puts her hands on her hips and stares at me. "Why are you smiling?"

I move toward her. She takes a step back, but I move to the left and continue past her. Straight to Travis. My arms wrap around him and pull him in for a hug. "How are you, man?"

"Good to see you, Billy. Heard you were back in town."

"Yeah. I was going to give you a call. I just wanted to get settled in first."

"Wait, you two know each other?" Sadie's voice is laced with irritation.

"Practically since we were born," Officer Travis replies.

"Ugh," she groans, throwing her hands up in the air. "Stupid small towns."

"You happen to live in this stupid small town," I remind her, not winning myself any points.

"Whatever, forget it. Just... don't be an asshole. You want to make noise? Do it after eight like any decent human being," she tells me before storming out of the house.

"How in the hell did you manage to piss her off when you've only been in town for five minutes?" Travis asks with a laugh.

"Talent," I say. Or pure fucking bad luck, which is exactly what I seem to have these days.

"She's been through a lot," Travis tells me. "Give her some time. I'm sure she'll warm up to you."

"I doubt that."

"Can I get you some coffee?" I ask, heading into the kitchen.

Travis checks his watch, then looks back at me with a smile. "It's New Hope. Aside from guys like you disturbing the peace, I have all the time in the world."

I pour him a cup and hand it to him before making my own. "Who would have thought that you of all people would have become a cop, let alone the assistant chief of police."

I recall many a time that Tommy would wreak havoc on this town. A little destruction here, a few pranks there. And I was always there to bail him out of trouble. Much the way Mason did for me.

"Yeah, well, I guess we all have to grow up sometime." He joins me at the table. "Sorry to hear about your knee. That must be hard."

"Wasn't exactly in my game plan," I tell him.

"That why you're here? Trying to figure out your next play?"

"Sort of. Trying to take back control. Trying to fix what's broken." I shrug. "I don't know. When everything happened, I just felt... lost. Coming back here was the only thing I could think of."

Travis looks around the old house. "Looks like you've got your work cut out for you."

"You can say that again."

"Well, I, for one, am glad you're back," Travis says.

"Yeah, I'm glad I'm back, too."

A call comes over the radio attached to Travis's shoulder. "I have to go. Looks like you're not the only trouble in town today. Certainly, the most welcome, though."

He gives me a hug and we make a promise to get together soon. When he's gone, I sit down on my couch. I wait for the moment that it turns eight and I crank up the sander. Along with every other noise making machine I have. If Sadie wants to play, she has no idea who she's playing against.

Chapter 10

Sadie

I groan at the fact that I'm that person. The one who is willing to struggle trying to juggle my ten grocery bags rather than make multiple trips. The proverbial work harder, not smarter. Not exactly the way it's supposed to go, but let's face it, nothing in my life has to date. Why start now?

"Need some help?" The sound of my overbearing, rude, intrusive asshole of a neighbor's voice simultaneously turns me on and pisses me off.

Opting to follow my anger vibe, I reply with a resounding, "No" as I make my way up the sidewalk to my front door. With every step, I can hear one of the bags ripping further and further.

"No, no, no. Just hold on for another minute." The whispered prayer is not answered and the bag tears some more.

"You sure?" I can hear the laughter in Billy's voice as he watches me struggle. Only, I'm not sure if he's laughing at my struggle or the fact that I'm refusing help when I clearly need it.

"I don't want anything from you," I tell him. Only then does fate decide to intervene and make me eat my words. The bag breaks, items spilling all over the yard as I struggle to keep the other bags from falling.

Out of the corner of my eyes, I can see Billy making his way toward me. "I'm fine. I don't need your help."

Anyone else? Sure, they can help all day. Just not him. Not today. Not after the phone conversation with Jon this morning, the woman who seemed to be moaning beneath him as I tried to speak to him about our son. Not Billy. Not now.

Just as everything threatens to crash, Billy's next to me, grabbing several of the bags before they fall. "Leave me alone. I don't need your help." I argue with him as I play tug of war with the bags.

"Jesus, you are the most stubborn woman I have ever met," he says as he fights to keep the bags from falling.

Everything hits the ground. Including us. Billy falls back with me landing on top of him with a thud. "Look what you did."

"Me?" He laughs. "I was just trying to help."

"I didn't need your help."

"Clearly." He continues to laugh, his head resting on the ground. "I haven't had this much fun in months."

"Fun? You call this fun?"

I press my hand to his extremely firm chest and push myself up.

He quirks an eyebrow at me. "A gorgeous woman straddling me? Damn right I call that fun."

Only then do I realize the position we're in. And a certain firmness that begins to press between my thighs. "Oh my God."

I jump up and as far away from him as I can.

"Sorry. It's been a while since, uh..." He shakes his head, ridding his mouth of whatever he was just about to say. Words that there is no way in hell I would believe. Him not have sex for a while? Please. Every woman in this town is already drooling over him. Stopping by to bring him baked goods that contain offers of more, I'm sure. "I'm sorry. Let me help you clean this up."

"You've done enough." I squat down and begin to gather the groceries that are scattered all about. As I do, laughter bubbles over, and tears sting my eyes.

"Sadie? You okay?"

"Do I look like I'm okay?"

Billy slowly makes his way to the ground, his hand resting on my back. "What is it?"

"You really want to know? Fine. I just got done with a twelve-hour shift where one of my patients nearly died. Then I got to have a really pleasant conversation with my ex while his new girlfriend moaned in the background. And now... this. I'm done. I've had it. I
—"

"It's going to be all right. I'll help—"

"Don't you get it? I don't want your help. I don't want you here. I just want to be left alone."

"I can't do that."

"Why not?"

"Because... not all guys walk away when things get tough. Some of them stick it out."

"I'm a mess."

"We're all a mess, Sadie." He rises to his feet and extends his hand to me. "It's nice when you have someone to help you clean it up, though." He helps me to my feet. "Get the door. I got these."

Once all the bags are settled in the kitchen, Billy makes his way to the front door without so much as a word.

"Billy, wait," I call after him.

"Uh-uh."

I turn my head to the side, confused by his nondescript word.

"If you thank me, it's going to ruin our whole dynamic."

"What are you talking about?"

"You hate me. I try to get you to like me. I'm having fun with it. Let's just let it roll."

"So, you want me to not like you?"

Another nonchalant shrug. "You need to not like me right now, for whatever reason. I'm okay with that."

"Still, you helped me today. I want to..."

He shakes his head.

"What?" I ask, becoming increasingly furious with him.

"You've had a rough day. I don't want you to say anything you might regret." Billy winks at me and turns to head out the door just as Jules is walking in.

"Well, isn't this cozy," she coos.

"Far from it," Billy says as he continues through the door and away from me. "Later, Jules."

"Did you scare him away?" Jules asks, her hands on her hips.

"No. Maybe? I don't know." The man makes no sense to me, nor does the conversation we just had. Yet, it was nice. He was nice. And that makes me even more on guard than I was before. "It doesn't matter."

Jules grabs a few items out of the bag. "Sadie, Sadie, Sadie."

"What, what, what?" I ask, mimicking her.

"Are you ever going to take off this suit of armor and trade it in for some sexy lingerie?"

"If I do, it won't be for him."

My eyes wander out the window and to the man who continues to work tirelessly on a house I would have deemed a lost cause days ago. Yet, there he is, sawing and hammering and nailing. And every word I can think of has my mind drifting back to the moment in the front yard when my body straddled his. The feeling of him pressing against me.

"But you're right. Maybe I do need to have a little fun."

Something to get my neighbor off my mind and get my libido back in check.

Jules claps her hands together. "Yes. Finally. Tomorrow night. Me. You. Available men."

Chapter 11

Billy

"I don't know," I tell Travis.

When he asked me to meet him for a beer, I had assumed it was to catch up. Not for him to try to rope me into something. Especially not football related.

"I came here to forget about football. Not be a part of it," I explain as I sit at the bar next to him with my water in my hand.

"I get that, I do. But you said you were looking for a purpose. Maybe that house isn't it. Maybe this is. Besides, think of all the good you'll do."

Apparently, at some point New Hope's junior football team fell apart. With no one to run it and no one to coach it, it just kind of faded into the dust.

"Even if I did... I can't coach all the teams." Realistically, I probably could. I have nothing but free time on my hands. Still, I don't want to be around football that much. Hell, I don't want to be around it at all.

"I can help coach," Travis says. "We just need... direction."

I raise an eyebrow. "Really? Because from what you've told me, you need a complete program."

"Did I mention I can help coach?" Travis repeats. "Come on, man, the kids..."

Travis's voice trails off. Curious to see what's caught his attention, I turn around. Jules. And much to my libido's pleasure, she's accompanied by Sadie. Sadie, who looks downright striking in her tight jeans and low-cut tank top.

Travis and I sit at the bar, both silenced by the beautiful women who just walked into the bar. One who seems pleased by it. The other? Furious.

"What are you staring at?" Sadie asks as she approaches us, her hands on her hips. Only this time, it's not me that her anger is directed at. It's Travis.

"Only the most beautiful woman this side of the equator." Travis's compliment couldn't be any more awful if he tried. Clearly, Jules seems to think so, too.

"Then maybe you shouldn't have screwed it up." Sadie's demeanor toward Travis is completely different from what it was this morning. Guess when the uniform comes off, the claws come out.

Me, on the other hand, I'm just grateful to not have her yelling at me for a change. All I need is more attention. The women who flocked to me the moment I stepped into the bar was more than enough. Each one wanted a piece of the football player. The man I no longer am. Each one was thoroughly disappointed when I sent them packing. Not that it stopped another from approaching.

"Eyes to yourself," she directs him. Then turns her attention to me. "Same goes for you."

"Yes, ma'am." I divert my eyes back to the bar with the smile. Despite her demands on my part, I can feel her eyes on me. Watching, waiting, wondering if I am going to disobey her. No way. If I stand a chance in hell of getting this woman to so much as tolerate me, I need to follow her orders. As I sit here, on my best behavior, the thought of what other kind of orders she might give me seep into my mind. If she only knew the lengths I would go to in order to please her. Finally satisfied that I've done as I was told, Sadie walks away.

"What did you do?" I ask Travis. Jules never made her way to the bar. Instead, she sat at a table and did her best to ignore the confrontation she clearly wanted no part of.

"Nothing."

"Come on, T, this is me. You can tell me."

"No, seriously. I didn't do anything. She's the one who dumped me."

"Well, yeah, I see that. Why, though?"

"Because she wanted to find herself. So, she ended things, left for college, then came back a whole different person. Fuck, man, I waited. I waited for her and when she came back, I thought that maybe we would... I don't know, get back together, I guess."

"Then why the hell is Sadie over here blaming you?"

"This all happened before Sadie moved to town. I can only imagine what kind of story Jules must have spun."

"Why in the hell are you letting her get away with it?" I won't. In fact, I'm going to put an end to this right now. I stand from my stool, ready to walk over to Sadie and Jules and give them a piece of my mind. Travis is quick to follow suit, but rather than moving, he presses his hand to my chest and begs me to sit down.

"I appreciate it, Billy, but it's not worth it. Besides—"

"Besides what? You can't just let people treat you like that." That's when I see the look on his face. "Holy shit, you still love her."

"Keep your voice down," he orders me. "Christ, I don't need the whole town knowing I'm pining away for some chick who hates me."

My dick and I feel his pain. Taking a quick glance in their direction, I nod to let him know I won't do anything to give him away.

Travis does an abrupt subject change. "So, about that football team. What do you say?"

"You're not going to give this up, are you?"

Travis shakes his head. "So?"

I let my head fall back with a sigh. "Fine. But... as repayment, you're going to have to help me with some shit around the house."

"Bit off more than you can chew?" Travis asks with a laugh.

"And then some. Whatever it is that I thought I knew about home restoration goes right out the window with this place." And all the shit is a lot harder than I remember. I'm not sure if it's my knee causing the issue, or maybe even my mind. Whatever it is, this project is progressing way slower and is proving much more difficult than I had anticipated. "Not to mention I didn't realize the place had fallen apart so much."

"Yeah, the people living there were something else. Got called to quite a few domestic calls for there." He takes a swig from his beer. "The last ones were the worst. Little girl, no more than three. Found her home alone one night. Had to be well after ten. Thank God for Sadie. She was at least able to comfort her until child services got there."

The guilt I had thought I had started to move past reemerges. Reminding myself I can't change the past; I allow myself to be glad that Bryce doesn't have to live next door to something like that anymore. I can only imagine what he saw—what he would still be seeing if I hadn't bought the house back.

"So, not only do I get my friend back, but you also cleaned up the town a little. See, that knee injury is doing some good."

With a roll of my eyes, I swivel in my chair and take in the atmosphere. "I already said yes. You don't have to keep kissing my ass."

My eyes land on the dance floor, which has become increasingly crowded as the night has progressed. Sadie and Jules are out there, twirling around and shaking their asses.

"Mesmerizing, isn't it?" Travis says, a longing look in his eyes. "Why don't you go dance with her?"

I shake my head. "Not a good idea. Besides, even if I did want to..." I tap on my knee. The tumble Sadie and I took the other day scared me enough. Luckily, everything was fine. Not even so much as an ounce of pain.

"Hi there." The sound of a sultry voice appears next to me. I turn my head, taking in the woman it belongs to. Shit.

"Hey, Faith."

Her fingers find their way to my arm, then slide to my chest. "Long time no see."

"Yep." My body stiffens at her unwanted touch.

As her fingers continue to graze my chest, she babbles on about what she's been up to. How sorry she is to hear about my injury. And then finishes with a, "I've missed you, Billy."

I bet she has.

How I had managed to avoid the woman this long is beyond me. I had been on such a roll, though; I was starting to hope that it would be a permanent reprieve. No such luck. The woman I lost my virginity to and my high school sweetheart, if you can call her that, is standing before me with all her glory hanging out.

Off to the side, I can hear Travis snickering. Some fucking friend.

"What do you say we get out of here? Maybe I can jog your memory about how good we are together?"

"That's a great offer, Faith, but, uh..."

As I try to come up with an excuse, I notice a table off to the side and the crowd that's gathered around it. Sadie stands on top of it, her hips swaying. My dick hardens instantly at the sight. Christ, she looks like the picture of perfection up there. Despite Faith's presence, my eyes are glued to Sadie. To her hips. To the way she moves. The already rowdy Saturday night crowd is hooting and hollering at her while Jules just stands there with a proud smile.

I admit, Sadie looks more relaxed and freer than I have ever seen her. She's having fun and deserves to, so I don't want to stop her. But I find myself getting irritated by the men looking at her.

"So, what do you say?" Faith asks.

"About what?" I reply.

"Are you kidding me? You're watching her when you could have this?"

Some guy hops up on the table with Sadie. At first, they just dance, and as much as I don't like it, Sadie seems to be okay with it. Then he touches her. Her waist, sliding down to her hips. She tries to shake him off, but he keeps going until he's pressing his body against hers.

Having had enough, I get out of my seat.

"Hey, Sadie," I call out as I stand at the table before her.

"Back off, man," the guy shouts. He's drunk and belligerent, so despite the massive size difference between him and me, he's not scared. However, when Travis steps up next to me, he backs down.

Sadie, on the other hand, is drunk in her own right and seems completely oblivious to anything but me. "What? You want a dance, Billy?"

The woman has no fucking clue just how fucking on point she is with that statement.

"Nope. Just want to get you home."

"Won't your date be upset about that?"

"She's not my date. You're the only one I'm interested in tonight, Sadie."

"Oh, really?" She jumps down from the table and lands haphazardly in my arms. "Then instead of taking me home... why don't you take me to your home?" I set her on the floor, my hands on her hips to steady her. Sadie runs her finger down my chest. "Jesus, you're unreal."

Fingers turn to hands and the way she's touching me is leaving me more than a little turned on. "Come on, Sadie, let's get you home."

"Your home," she argues.

"Fine, my home." The one right next door to hers. The one that if she weren't so drunk right now, is the exact place that I would want to take her. But I can't. I'm not that guy. Christ, I wish I were right now.

Pleased with my response, Sadie grabs my face and kisses me. My mind tells me to stop the kiss. To take the drunk girl home and put her to bed. My hands and my dick have other thoughts. I kiss her back, my tongue dancing with hers as my hands slide from her hips to her ass. If it weren't illegal, I would take her right here. Right now.

Only problem is the girl is drunk. Beyond drunk. So drunk that I'm fairly certain she doesn't even know it's me she's kissing.

When we pull away, though, her glossy eyes lock with mine. She stares at me, looking oddly sober, before kissing me again.

"We should probably take this home," I suggest when every fiber of my being is telling me to pull her into the storage closet and give her exactly what she's asking for.

Her eyes twinkle at the suggestion, her voice eager. "Let's go."

The moment I begin to drive us away, I glance over at her in the passenger seat. I expect to see her passed out or pissed off, but instead she's full of life. She's dancing in the seat, a huge smile on her face. "That is so not like me."

"Which part?"

"All of it. The drinking, the dancing. The kissing." She touches her fingers to her lips. "I can't believe I kissed you."

"That makes two of us," I mumble. The effects of that kiss strain against my jeans. "So, what are you saying, Sadie? Do I bring out the bad in you?"

"That kiss was anything but bad."

"Probably even be better if you were sober."

"Is that a dare?"

"A dare?" I ask, confused.

"Are you daring me to kiss you when I'm sober?"

"Not daring. Hoping."

"You want me to kiss you?" She turns in her seat to face me.

"Truth?" She nods. "I want to do a hell of a lot more than just kiss you."

"What about Faith? It looked like she wanted to kiss you."

"I'm not interested in Faith."

"But you're interested in me?"

"Unfortunately."

Her face falls at my response.

"No man wants to be infatuated with a woman who won't give him the time of day."

"Which is the precise reason I think you want her. Because she doesn't want you."

"Despite what people think, plenty of women don't want me."

Sadie scoffs at the comment. "Oh, please."

"It's true. Since we're asking questions here, why is it exactly that you don't want me? Or even like me for that matter?"

"Because you're a man. I can't... I won't let someone break my heart again. And I sure as hell am not going to let someone in who's just going to leave and hurt Bryce."

I nod. The by-product of a broken home, I completely get where she's coming from. My mother had been the same way for years.

When I pull up in front of the house—her house—I walk around the car and open the door for her. With her hand in mine, she steps from the vehicle. We step onto her porch, and she leans against the door. "You know, I'm kind of sober now."

"Sadie..." My restraint is wearing thin. This being a good guy gig can wear thin on a man. Especially a man who desperately wants what's right in front of him. How in the fuck am I supposed to resist her when she's so damn willing?

"Just... a kiss. I've never been kissed like that before, and I doubt I will be again."

"Kissed like what?" I ask, ego and curiosity getting the best of me.

"So thoroughly. So completely. So... damn good."

Fucking hell, this woman makes me do things I normally wouldn't do. Against my better judgment, I caress her cheek with my hand as I press my lips to hers. Hard, slow, full of fucking emotion that I wish to God I wasn't feeling.

"Good night, Sadie."

"Night, Billy."

Chapter 12

Billy

"What ya doin'?" a small voice asks from behind me.

I smile, knowing it's Bryce. "Does your mom know you're over here?"

I ask the question because the last thing I want is to get on Sadie's bad side again. Sure, she's been avoiding me like the plague since our drunken kiss the other night, but I still feel like we made progress. If she remembers any of it, that is.

"Yep," Bryce replies.

"Really?"

He nods eagerly. "Can we hang out now?"

"Sure," I say skeptically. I nod toward his front yard, and we move in that direction. I'm not taking any chances at this point. Sitting down in the grass with him in his yard and me in mine, I show him the football plans I had been putting together.

"I love football," he tells me, his face lighting up. "I'm even having a football birthday party. Will you come? All the kids will be so jealous. And my dad will be so surprised."

"Your dad is coming?"

Bryce shrugs. "I hope so, but Mom told me not to get my hopes up because he's super busy."

Yeah, I bet he is. I don't even know the guy and I already hate him. What kind of asshole leaves his wife and kid? My attention turns back to Bryce, who's looking at the playbook I'm putting together.

"These look so cool."

"Well, you should join then."

"Mom doesn't like football. I don't think she'll let me."

"Well, football can be dangerous." I point to my now defunct knee. "I can understand why she wouldn't want you to play."

"It's not that," he says as he picks at the grass.

"What is it then?"

"My dad. He likes football. He taught me all about it. And Mom... well, she doesn't like anything to do with Dad anymore."

"I'm sure if you talked to her about it."

He shakes his head adamantly. "She made me promise to clean my room every day for a whole year just to have the football party. I can't imagine what she would make me do to play."

Biting back the chuckle that threatens at his rationale, I make him an offer. "You want me to talk to her for you?"

"You would do that?"

"I would. But that doesn't mean I'm going to change her mind." If anything, it might make the situation worse. "I'll talk to her, but if she says no, then that's it."

"Deal," Bryce says, extending his hand to me.

"Bryce," Sadie's voice yells from the door.

"Go," I whisper. "Before you get me in trouble." I throw in a wink, so he knows I'm just kidding.

Off he goes with a giddy smile on his face. Sadie stands in the doorway a minute longer, staring at me and shaking her head. I'm not really sure what to make of it. Of her. Maybe that's it. Maybe she's trying to figure me out, the same way I am her.

Before she can close the door, I call out her name. She stops but doesn't turn around.

"Can we talk for a minute?"

She steps outside the door but doesn't leave her porch. She doesn't speak, only looks at me. Definitely a far cry from the woman who told me she had never been kissed as thoroughly, or as good, as I kissed her.

Closing the gap between us, I walk toward her and stop at the steps.

"I was just talking to Bryce."

"Despite me telling you to leave him alone?"

I shrug. "What can I say? The kid loves me." Sadie doesn't seem to find the humor in it that I do. "And he told me that you said it was okay."

She purses her lips together, hiding her smile. "Outside. In the yard. No going in the house. Understood?"

"Yes, ma'am." I agree to her request in the same manner I did the other night.

"You wanted to talk?"

I nod. "I told Bryce that I would talk to you, but that if you say no, then that's it."

"Talk to me about what?" She angles her head as she gives me a very concerned look.

"Travis and I are putting together a youth football program and —"

"Stop right there." She holds her hand out in front of her and shakes her head. "The answer is no."

"But—"

"No."

"Will you just let me speak?" I argue with her even though I know I shouldn't.

She crosses her arms across her chest. "Fine. Go ahead."

I move up to the first step so that we're eye to eye. "Bryce told me you're not a football fan. He also told me why. And I get it, I do, but... I think this is a really great opportunity for him."

Sadie laughs. "Because you know him so well?"

"Yeah, maybe I do. Maybe I know how he feels. Football saved me from being one screwed up kid. It gave me something positive to focus on rather than all the negatives."

"Bryce has plenty of positives in his life."

"Except a dad." I know the moment the words came out of my mouth that I fucked up. It was the wrong thing to say. The wrong person to say it to. If only I could take it back, but I can't. So instead, I try to explain my stupidity away. "I know what it's like. I've been in his shoes. My dad left me, too. And I think that—"

"Did your dad leave you to follow some stupid sport around? Did he make you less of a priority than your own kid because football is life?"

"Well, no. But—"

"Then you don't know. And you don't understand. I am not going to allow him to play some sport just because he thinks it will bring his father back. He already roped me into this stupid football themed birthday party. I won't do this." She paused for a moment.

"And I would really appreciate it if you would mind your own business."

This right here is why I played football. I was shit at baseball, always striking out. Just like I am with Sadie. The worst part is, when it comes to her, I don't want to give up.

"That's not what you said the other night."

I throw the vivid memory of her lips on mine in front of her.

"I was drunk."

"Funny, you swore to me you weren't. In fact, you told me that you wanted to—"

She clamps her hand over my mouth. "Shhh. I was drunk. It was a mistake. Nothing more."

I press my lips to her palm. She might be trying to hide it, but I can hear the gasp escape her when I do.

"Think what you want, but deep down, we both know the truth."

"Which is?"

"Had I not been a gentleman, I could have had whatever I wanted." Just for good measure, I throw in, "And believe me, Sadie, I wanted it. So bad." I jog down the steps. "If you change your mind about letting Bryce play, you know where to find me."

***

My muscles ache and my head is pounding. I've been putting in overtime on the house, trying desperately to make some headway with it. With way more left to get done than I would like there to be, I decide to take a break and head to the coffee shop, hoping that between the walk and the caffeine I get slightly reenergized.

The moment I walk in the door, I'm slapped in the face with a visual of Sadie bending over. She's picking up the napkin she dropped on the floor. I'm eternally grateful to the woman for choosing to bend at the waist rather than squat down. Absolute perfection.

She must be able to feel my gaze on her because the moment she stands, her head whips in my direction. The glare she gives me is undeniable and also sexy as hell. I've never found someone disliking me so damn attractive before, let alone such a turn-on. I give her a quick wink before heading to the counter.

"Oh my gosh, you're so hot," the barista blurts out. Her face flushes a bright shade of red as she drops her gaze from me to the register. "What can I get you?"

"Black coffee, four stevia," I tell her. "And thank you for the compliment." The whole while I'm interacting with the young woman, I make sure to keep an eye on my gorgeous neighbor. From what I can tell, she seems to be trying to convince Jules to take their coffee to go. Lucky for me, Jules doesn't seem to want to.

"He had the nerve to insinuate that I'm going to screw Bryce up if I don't let him join this stupid football league," Sadie tells Jules, not realizing I'm now standing next to her.

"Actually," I say when I've made my way over to them. She jumps in her seat, her hand flying to her chest as I continue on. "I said that football saved me from being a screwed-up kid. Me, not Bryce. I'm sorry if I offended you, Sadie, which wasn't my intention. Bryce told me he loves football, and he wants to join the league. I thought it would give him something to focus his energy on this summer. And me, too."

"I don't need you to take care of my son for me." Sadie stands from her seat and stares at me.

"Quit twisting my words. That's not what I'm doing. I just wanted to help."

"Yeah, well, you're doing the complete opposite." Without another word, Sadie turns on her heel and exits the coffee shop.

Leaving my coffee behind, I storm out of the coffee shop and onto the sidewalk. "Why are you so hell-bent on keeping Bryce away from football? Or is it just me you want to keep him away from?"

"Because I don't want his heart to get broken."

"I have no intention of doing that."

"Maybe not, but once you get over whatever has you hibernating here, Bryce won't be anything more than an afterthought. Which is fine, except that he's already had someone important walk out of his life and not look back. He doesn't deserve to go through that again."

"No, he doesn't. I get why you're protective. But that doesn't give you the right to make assumptions about me. I wouldn't do that. I'm not that guy, Sadie."

"I didn't think his father was either. Yet here we are."

I close the distance between us, my thumb gently wiping away the tear that fell unwillingly. "I'm sorry he hurt you. I'm sorry he hurt Bryce."

That's it. I say nothing more as we stand there in the middle of the sidewalk. She rests her cheek in my hand and takes the small amount of comfort that I'm able to offer her. It only lasts a moment; nothing more, nothing less. Long enough to intrigue me more and for her to come to her senses.

"I-I have to go."

A moment later, Jules is at my side. "Nice work. You're breaking down her defenses."

"I'm being nice, Jules. Remember I'm a nice guy?"

"Thought he went out the window when your football career did?" She throws my words back in my face.

"Yeah, well, maybe that realtor of mine is smarter than she lets on. Looks like my neighbor brought me back to life." Jules has a cocky grin on her face. "Now if only said realtor would get out of her own way and give Travis a shot."

The smile drops immediately. "How dare you."

"Payback, sweetheart."

I jog off to catch up to Sadie. I'm not letting her get away this time.

"Can we not do this?"

"I don't know what you're talking about."

"One minute you're kissing me, the next you're screaming at me. Both are hot as hell, but still. I'm starting to get whiplash here. Why are you so dead set on disliking me?"

"I already told you. You're a man. You exist. That's enough for me."

"I might be a man, but I'm not him."

That got her attention. Sadie stops dead in her tracks and turns to me. "Excuse me?"

"I'm pretty sure you heard me." I continue walking past her. Now it's her turn to follow me. I can hear the clicking of her heels on the pavement behind me.

"Whatever it is that you think you know, you have no idea."

"And whatever judgment you're passing on me for having a dick, you couldn't be more wrong."

Chapter 13

Billy

I'm directing Travis and a couple of his coworkers, Dallas and Chad, on how we're going to run the teams. The kids all sit anxiously on the fifty-yard line of the high school football field.

As I speak, I feel a tug on the bottom of my shirt. When I turn, I find Bryce standing there.

"What are you doing here?" I ask, fearing what Sadie would say, or do, if she knew.

Proudly, he hands me a piece of paper. "She signed it."

I glance down at the paper. I don't know Sadie's handwriting, but it looks legit. At least it doesn't look like he signed it. Something tells me I should check on this. Part of me, though, hopes that maybe I got through to her.

Travis grabs the slip from my hand and tells Bryce to go sit with the other kids. He runs to where his friend Tommy is sitting and plops down.

"I don't know, man."

Travis shrugs. "Afraid of making Sadie mad?"

"Damn right I am. You've seen her when she's pissed."

"Listen, the kid has a signed slip. What are we supposed to do? Say we don't trust him?" Travis grabs the red scrimmage vests. "I say we let him play and if she has an issue with it, tell her it was my decision. I'm used to her hating me."

"Don't think I won't throw your ass under the bus," I joke.

"I'm counting on in." He moves in close and lowers his voice. "As long as you promise me that you're going to try and hit that."

I give Travis a shove toward the field and refuse to answer his question. For now, I'm going to take his word for it. I'll suffer the consequences later if need be.

Letting Travis and Dallas run the show while I sit on the sidelines and observe is a tough task. It was one of the hardest things I did post-surgery—sit on the sidelines. I hate not being in the action. While this time I'm on the sidelines with the purpose of gauging the kids, it still feels familiar.

My spirit picks up when I watch Bryce catch a ball that Travis throws. Definitely a tougher pass than I would make to a seven-year-old kid, but Bryce caught it. In fact, he gave Travis quite a run when he tossed it back to him. The kid has an arm on him. He might just be our new QB.

Once I finally have a good handle on the kids and their abilities, we begin to run a few drills. While most are floundering around, I find myself awestruck by Bryce. He's really giving it his all and doing a damn good job.

The moment that practice ends, Bryce runs up to me. "So, how'd I do?"

I ruffle his sweaty hair. "You did great, kid. I was really impressed."

He stands there, smiling from ear to ear. "I watched all your old videos last night trying to get ready for today."

"It shows," I tell him, hiding my laughter. This is the most excited and animated I have ever seen him. No way do I want to diminish any of that.

"Do you think we could practice more tonight? I really want to be good for the first game."

"How about tomorrow?" I suggest. "I need to get some work done on the house."

"Can I help?"

"You know your mom wouldn't like that." He nods in agreement. "I'm surprised she even let you join."

"Tommy's waiting. I have to go. See ya, Billy."

"See ya, Bryce," I say as I watch him run away.

***

Stepping into my bathroom, I pull my shirt over my head and discard it on the floor. It's been a long day and my knee is killing me. I'm dying for a hot shower, something to ease the discomfort and relax my mind. And my newfound guilt. The more and more I think about it, the less I believe that Sadie signed that slip.

By the time I step in the shower, the water cascading over me, my thoughts are less about the permission slip and more about Sadie. About what she does to me, how she makes me feel. Her kiss. That fucking kiss that blew my mind. Her lips felt like heaven, her body a damn sin.

The thought alone has me all riled up. Tension coils in my balls and before I can even realize what I'm doing, my hand is stroking my cock. Wrong. So wrong. Her eyes. That mouth. The verbal lashings. Fuck, Sadie. So damn perfect. I can practically see her before me, hands splayed on the shower wall, her ass grinding against my hips as my cock drives into her. The sounds, so much deeper and fierce than during our kiss the other night. I can see it. I can feel it. So good. So real. Cum shoots out onto the wall, my hand, the tile floor. The orgasm releasing so much pressure in me. Relief. Happiness. Completion.

Resting my hand against the shower wall, my head hung, I fall prey to the feeling. I allow it to consume me. For the first time in months, I feel good. And while it may have been months of pent-up orgasms that brought it to fruition, there is only one woman in all this time that made that a possibility.

Sadie.

My Sadie.

I can try and deny it all I want, but it's no use. I want her. Not just sexually, either. Though I sure as hell want that. Still, there are no ifs, ands, or buts about it—I'm falling for her. Now I just need to figure out a way to make her hate me a little less and like me a little more.

The distinct sound of pounding on the steel door breaks through my thoughts. Grabbing a towel off the rack, I wrap it around my waist and head to the front door.

"I'm coming," I shout as I pad through the living room.

I'm not exactly sure who I expected to be on the other side of the door. It sure as hell wasn't Sadie. Certainly not a very pissed Sadie. Though I'm pretty sure I know exactly what she's so pissed about this time.

"How dare you?" she shouts.

Chapter 14

Sadie

The moment the words fall from my lips, my mouth goes dry. The sight of Billy standing before me in nothing but a towel, his bare chest dripping wet, is more beautiful than I imagined it would be. My hands ache to run over the hard planes of his body, the ripples of the six pack and straight down that sexy V that dips into the towel.

"How dare I what?" he asks.

His voice brings me back to the present and the reason I came over here to begin with. My eyes might be taking him in, but my head is focused on my anger once again.

"As if you don't know. I told you I didn't want Bryce playing football and yet you let him on the team anyway," I shout, tossing the uniform I found under Bryce's bed at his dripping chest.

"I would never let Bryce on the team without authorization."

"Clearly, I didn't authorize it."

"Someone did," he says before moving back into his house. "I'll be right back."

Uninvited, I step inside, following him. I'm so focused on watching the way the muscles on his back move that I don't realize he's stopped, and I slam right into him.

"You okay?" he asks, his head turned back toward me and a smile on his face.

Damn this man and the looks on his face. Ones that seem so genuine and true that they make me want to melt, to get to know him. To not be angry with him.

Allowing my hands the pleasure to feel the firm warmth of his skin beneath them for a moment longer before removing them and stepping back.

"You could have warned me."

"I don't remember inviting you in," he says.

I can't even argue because he's right. He didn't. And this isn't the first time I've stormed into his house without invitation. Yet, he never seems fazed by it despite the fact that all I do is give him hell.

"I'm sorry."

"Don't be."

He hands me a sheet of paper. "What's this?"

"Bryce's signed permission slip."

I look down at the form, the one I told him in no uncertain terms I wouldn't sign. No doubt as I look at it that there's a signature on it, though. It just isn't mine. The big, loopy handwriting means there is only one person to blame for this. Jules.

"I didn't sign this."

"Yeah, well, it's your name and he said you did."

He said I did. I close my eyes at the realization that my not even eight-year-old son lied and forged my signature. Well, had it forged.

"He is not playing." I tear up the form and let the pieces fall to the floor.

"Okay."

"Okay?"

"Yeah, okay. I respect your decision. If you don't want Bryce to play, he won't play."

"You'll respect it, but you don't agree with it, do you?"

"I don't, no. But my opinion doesn't mean shit." He reaches for the door handle. "If that's settled, can I go put some clothes on now?"

It's a sin for the man to be clothed when he looks like that. "Yes, of course." Embarrassed, I turn and hurry down the steps. "Hey, Billy?"

"Yeah?"

"How'd he do today?"

"If you hadn't ripped up that slip, I was going to make him the quarterback. He's good, Sadie. Damn good."

I give him a subtle nod and head back home. On my way across the yard, I notice Jules's car parked in front of the house. I groan upon sight, knowing that she's going to give me shit the moment I set foot inside.

"So, what were you doing over at Billy's house?" Jules wiggles her eyebrows at me.

"What else? Arguing," I reply as I plop onto the couch.

"There is plenty you should be doing with Billy that involves your mouth. Arguing is not one of them."

I pick up the pillow next to me and throw it at her. "Sometimes I wonder how we even became friends. Speaking of..."

She looks at me innocently.

"How dare you sign that permission slip when you knew I didn't want Bryce playing?"

There's a knock on the door. Desperate to get herself out of trouble, Jules jumps up to grab it.

"Well, well, well, if it isn't my favorite client." Even though she's standing in the doorway, blocking my view, I know exactly who she's talking to.

"Is Sadie here?" The deep, rugged sound of his voice rustles over me and makes my skin tingle.

"Right here," I say as I make my way to the door.

Jules stands between us with a smirk on her perfect lips.

"Can you give us a minute?" I say, trying to urge her to go away.

"Why? Something I can't hear?" she teases.

"Nothing like that," Billy tells her. "I just wanted to see if you would let me break the news to Bryce."

"Break what news?" Jules asks.

"Really? The news that despite his aunt Jules going against my wishes, he isn't playing football," I growl at her before turning back to Billy. "You don't have to do that."

"I want to. Really, Sadie. Please?"

I step out of his way and allow him to enter my home. I nod in the direction of the stairs. "He's in his room. Second door on the left."

"Thanks."

I can't take my eyes off Billy as he trudges up the stairs, favoring his right knee slightly.

"What?" I ask, able to feel Jules's eyes on me.

"You're starting to fall for him."

"I am not," I scoff at the comment.

I head to the kitchen, anything to not have to face her and her prying eyes. Eyes that can see straight through me.

"Bullshit. You're letting him around Bryce. You're softening."

"I'm being nice. There's no sense in being at odds with our neighbor."

"You would have no problem being at odds with your neighbor if he didn't look like Billy." I shake my head. "Look me in the eye and tell me I'm wrong."

I face Jules, my hands gripping the sink behind me. Lifting my chin with defiance, I open my mouth and say, "I hate you."

She begins to dance around the kitchen, knowing she's right.

"He's attractive. And yes, if things were different, it might be fun to enjoy some... extra-curricular activities with him. But it's not going to happen."

Billy appears in the doorway a moment later and I hope to God he didn't hear our conversation.

There's a smile on his face, but it doesn't reach his eyes. "All good. I let him know." He looks between me and Jules. "Night, ladies."

Jules jerks her head in the direction of the living room, telling me to follow him. Against my better judgment, I do.

"I really appreciate you talking to him," I say.

Billy stops and turns to me. "I didn't want him to be angry with you when you're just doing what you think is best. He's a little upset, but he should be back to himself by tomorrow."

"Than—"

Billy presses a finger to my lips and shakes his head. He gives me a wink, one that's meant to be playful but sends an ache straight to my core, before heading out.

"You know, if you just fucked him already, you wouldn't have to change your panties every five minutes."

I grab the nearest pillow and chuck it at Jules.

Chapter 15

Sadie

The whole pediatric floor is in chaos. Kids are screaming; lights from cameras are flashing. That must mean our special guest has arrived. Our special guest who, until now, has remained top secret.

Stepping out of the nurses' station, I glance down the crowded hallway. Parents and children alike line the area. When my eyes fall on the man at the center of it all, I'm stunned. Billy.

He crouches down next to one of the kids. The little boy throws his arms around Billy's neck. His smile is broad and covers the entirety of his face. My eyes are glued to the scene before me and the genuine smile that covers Billy's face as he hugs the little boy back. Where most of the special guests we have come in and do their due diligence, for Billy it's so much more. He seems more in his element in this moment than any other time I have seen him over the past few weeks. He is loving bringing joy to these kids. The same way he does with Bryce.

Ever since he had his little chat with Bryce, I haven't been able to stop visualizing what it would have looked like. Billy sitting on the bed next to him, his arm around him. Maybe kneeling in front of him, despite his bad knee? The look of adoration in Bryce's eyes despite the bad news he was being given. The idea of it alone makes my heart skip a beat. For the love of God, the man is breathtaking and seeing him with my son puts him on a whole other level. Not to mention that Bryce never so much as mentioned not being able to play. He apologized for lying, gave me a hug, and that was it. We went back to life as normal.

"Be still, my heart, and soak my panties," Holly says as she comes to a stop next to me. "I can't believe you live next door to him and leave the house. I would just stare at him all day. Why have you not hooked up with him yet?"

"Because the man is a..." A what? A damn saint despite my actions. Here he is with a bunch of sick kids trying to make their day when for the past few weeks, he's done the same with my own son. For no reason other than the kindness of his heart. Yet, I've spent this whole time hating him. Or, at least, that's what I tell myself I've been doing.

Every look. Every moment. It just gets harder to dislike the man.

I sigh. "It's not like it matters. Even if I wanted to, there is no way that some rich, super-hot football player is going to want me."

Holly chews on her pen as she continues to stare at Billy. "I wouldn't be so sure about that if I were you. If the way he's looking at you is any indication, he wants you. Bad."

The gaze I had been trying to keep diverted from his turns in his direction and meets his. It can't be me he's looking at like that, can it? But there's no one else standing here. Holly moved to tend to one of the kids and left me eye locked with Billy.

While it feels like an eternity, it's only a few moments before one of the kids pulls his attention away from me. I'm grateful for the reprieve because that look, his face, it damn near had me buckling at the knees.

The woman standing behind him looks pleased, too. Based on her frenzied motions and high-strung demeanor, I can only assume that she's his publicist, the woman who set this up. As much as I hate it, I give her a once-over. She's tall and thin and gorgeous. Exactly the type of woman I would expect Billy to be with. And now, I hate her. Without reason. Much the way I found myself hating Billy these past few weeks.

It wasn't Billy I was angry with. It was me. I'm the one who lost her kid. I'm the one who failed as a mother. Billy didn't do that. He just tried to be nice. Like he said.

Out of the corner of my eye, I see a small figure in a doorway. Jack.

He's clutching to the wall, his body too weak to stand for long. My heart breaks for him. He tries so hard to be strong, to ignore that time for him is wearing thin. I do the same. Jack's been my buddy since I first started here—my favorite patient, even though I know I shouldn't play favorites.

My feet move toward Jack as I see his grip on the doorframe slipping. I'm on my knees, propping him up within moments. "Do you know him?"

He nods. "He's my favorite."

"Yeah?"

"Billy Saint is the best football player I've ever seen. I would give anything to meet him."

"Then why don't we get out there?"

Jack shakes his head. "I'm too weak. I don't want to bother everyone else."

"You are no bother," I try to assure him.

"Nah, I think I'd rather just go back to bed."

"Are you sure?"

He nods and I begrudgingly help him back to the bed rather than the nearby wheelchair. Once I have him settled, I make my way over to Billy and throw the biggest smile I can muster in his direction.

"Uh-oh. Looks like I'm in trouble with Nurse Sadie," he says.

The kids look between the two of us and giggle.

"Not even close. I hate to interrupt, but can we talk for a second?"

"Yeah, of course." He comes closer until his hand comes to rest on my back. "Is everything okay?"

I nod toward a quiet hallway. "Everything's fine. It's just..." He looks at me intently, waiting for my next words. "There's this kid. He's really sick and pretty shy. Things aren't looking good for him. You're his favorite football player, but he won't come out of his room, and I was just hoping that—"

Billy presses his finger to my lips. "Which room?"

I point in the direction. "His name is Jack."

Billy turns to the woman who accompanied him here and waves her over. "Can you get me one of everything and bring it to that room?"

"Billy, honey, our time is up. We should get going," the woman tells him.

"We'll go when I'm done. Please get me what I asked for." His words are matter-of-fact and the woman turns away in a huff to do as he asks. Then Billy disappears in the opposite direction. The direction of Jack's room.

My curiosity gets the best of me and I creep my way over until I'm standing outside of Jack's door. I shouldn't eavesdrop. I just want this to go well for him. And, if I'm honest, I want to see Billy in action. All I had been able to do until now was watch from a distance. I couldn't actually hear the interactions and now I get an up-close look at it.

"Hey there," Billy says. "You must be Jack."

While I can't see his face, I can picture the look on it. The one of pure amazement and awe.

"My name is Billy, just in case you didn't know."

"Not know?" Jack exclaims. "You're the best. You're... wow."

"Thanks. It's nice to hear that." Billy says it as though he didn't just hear it several dozen times moments before. "With my knee being messed up, I don't quite feel like the best anymore."

"I know what you mean. I used to be the best at baseball, but I can't do that anymore."

"You can't do it right now," Billy tells him. "Never say never. That's what my mom always told me."

"Maybe you can play again then." The excitement in Jack's voice is off the charts.

"Here's the thing. I could play again. But if I get hit the wrong way, I could completely blow out my knee, end up in a wheelchair. I made a choice not to play. You can make a choice to play again."

"Never say never," Jack repeats.

The woman who accompanied Billy here breezes past me, her shoulder bumping mine as she does. Without an apology, she continues on into Jack's room. "Here you go, Billy."

"Thanks, Tara. I appreciate you hanging around, but I think I've got it from here."

"Oh, it's no problem. I thought we could grab dinner, catch up." Ugh. She is so insanely obvious that it's not even funny.

Even better is the fact that Billy shoots her offer down. Flat. "I can't. I have plans tonight. And you have a plane to catch. Maybe next time I'm in New York."

Just as quickly as she blew into the room, she exits it. Not without stopping to have her say, though. Not that I'm entirely sure why she feels the need in the first place.

"He can do better than you," she tells me.

"Thanks, Tara," I reply. "Looks like he's already doing better than you and he's single."

I don't know why I bother to validate the woman and her comment in the slightest. It's not as though I'm interested in Billy. Nor is he interested in me. Still, the attitude she's exuding is infuriating in itself. Clearly, the woman needs to be put in place and I am more than happy to do it.

She storms away and I hate that I've missed so much of Jack and Billy's conversation. In fact, I missed enough that I didn't even see him exit the room.

Billy leans against the jamb of the door, a smile on his face. I wait for the teasing or taunting to start, but instead he says, "He's a great kid."

I nod in agreement. "That he is. Quite a stack of stuff you gave him."

Billy shrugs. "It's just stuff."

"With your signature on it, it's valuable stuff."

Another shrug.

"Thank you, again. For all of this, really. I haven't seen these kids this happy in a long time."

"Glad I could brighten their day. I'm happy to do it anytime if you think it will help. Just say the word."

Unsure what to say or do, we both just stand there awkwardly. It isn't until he says goodbye and begins to part ways with me that I realize what it is I want to say to him.

"Billy, wait." Billy comes to a halt.

"Bryce can play."

"Yeah?"

"Yeah. Under one condition."

"That I quit renovating at six in the morning?"

"That, too. But no. You need to be his coach. I want him on your team."

"I wouldn't have it any other way."

"Thanks again. For everything."

"You bet."

Chapter 16

Billy

"Fuck," I scream the word out at the top of my lungs. Certain the whole neighborhood heard me, I do my best to get up from the ground. Fucking bullshit knee.

"Oh my God, Billy? Are you okay?" Out of the corner of my eye, I can see Sadie rushing to my side to help me. The moment her hands touch me, I shove her away.

"I'm fine. Go away."

"I just want to help."

"I don't need your help and I sure as hell don't need you to play nurse to me." Pain that should only be affecting my knee radiates through my entire body and is topped with massive guilt. "I'm sorry."

"It's okay. Let's just get you up."

Her hands touch me again, only this time her touch doesn't instill anger; it makes me want her. Even more than I already do. There's not a lot she can do to help me get up, but her touch is encouragement enough.

"Thanks," I tell her once I'm on my feet again.

She nods. "Want me to check it out for you?"

I shake my head. "No, I'm good. It just locks up sometimes." He pauses, his gaze dropping to the ground. "I'm sorry about—"

"Don't apologize. I get it."

"I appreciate that, but you didn't deserve that."

She gives me a nonchalant shrug. "I'm a mom and a nurse. I've dealt with worse."

I slowly maneuver to the porch and take a seat on the swing. "You shouldn't have to. Especially not from me. I just... I'm trying, but some days I still struggle. The pain, the anger, the self-pity. It's better than it was. Christ, before I came here..." I shake my head in disbelief. Not only because of how much things have changed since I laid eyes on her, but the fact that I'm telling her any of this. "I was a complete mess. All I did was rehab my knee and drink myself into oblivion. Sometimes I even drank during my rehab sessions."

"You don't look any worse for the wear," she says as she joins me on the swing.

"I am, believe me. I still don't feel like myself. Like, this injury, the inability to play football anymore—it changed me permanently."

"I know how you feel," I admit. "My divorce makes me feel like that. Like I'm not good enough. Nothing more than a shell of the person I used to be."

"You look pretty damn good to me." I gently bump my shoulder against hers. Part of me wants to deflect the conversation from myself and the other part of me just can't resist telling her how badly I want her anymore.

Her cheeks flush at the compliment and I don't think I've ever seen her look more beautiful. "I don't need the ego boost. I know who I am, what I am. I'm happy with that. It's just..."

"What does that even mean?" I ask.

"I'm a divorced mom with stretch marks. I'm damaged goods. Certainly not the woman guys are banging down the door for a chance with. And I'm okay with that."

As if her description of herself isn't comical enough, the fact that she doesn't think men want her has me full-blown laughing.

"What's so funny?"

"Is that really how you see yourself?"

She looks down at her hands. "Maybe."

"Want to know what I see?"

"No."

I laugh again. "I see a strong, sexy woman. A MILF if you will."

"Oh my God." She gasps before doubling over in laughter. "I cannot believe you just called me that."

"Why not? You are. Just because you're a mom, Sadie, that doesn't make you any less attractive. And just because you're divorced, that doesn't mean you're damaged. It means your ex is an idiot."

"Billy..."

"I mean it, Sadie. You're amazing."

She clears her throat, a way to cleanse us of the current conversation in order to return to something she's more comfortable with. "How's your knee?"

"Can't handle the truth?"

"We were talking about you. Not me. So, don't pass the buck."

"It's feeling better, thank you."

"You should get inside. Elevate it. Put some ice on it."

"Want to join me, Nurse?"

"I thought you didn't need my nursing skills?"

"I don't. But maybe—just maybe—I need you."

"I think I hear Bryce calling," she lies.

Before she can get off the swing, I take hold of her hand. Her eyes flash toward me, wide and bright. A clear indication that she feels the same spark in this touch that I do.

"Any chance you'll come to practice today?" She bites her lip. At least she's thinking about it. "Bryce would love to have you there." I pause, "I would, too."

"I'll think about it."

"I'll take it."

***

After spending the morning icing my knee, I head to practice. And what a practice it is. A comedy of errors is more like it. It's taking everything in me to contain my laughter. Travis is having a hell of a time running this drill. The kids have lost focus. They're running amuck.

Except for Bryce. He's standing there, ready to work. I couldn't be prouder.

"Looks like you could use one of these," a sweet voice says.

I turn to see Sadie standing next to me. She hands me a steaming cup of coffee. A caffeine refill isn't necessary but appreciated. "Thanks."

I watch as Travis makes another attempt at getting the kids to line up.

"You're welcome." Everything about her seems different. Her voice, the way she reacts to me. She seems nervous and unsure as she stands there shifting from foot to foot. "How's he doing?"

"He's doing great," I tell her.

"Really?" She sounds surprised. The thing is. Out of all the kids, Bryce really is the best of them. I'm not sure if it's innate talent or the sheer desire to make people happy, but the kid is working his ass off and doing a damn good job at it, too. "Thank you."

"What are you thanking me for?" I ask, taking a sip of my coffee.

"Not giving up. Making me see past my anger at my ex and letting Bryce join."

"I did all that? Here I thought I just proved I wasn't some child predator."

"You still have a tendency to invite little kids into your home, so I'm not ruling it out."

"Not kids. Your kid. And Bryce, well, he happens to be my friend, so..." I stick out my tongue at her.

"I still don't like you," she says, which only tells me that she kind of, sort of does.

We stand there, taking in the scene before us. The practice I had been observing before stepping in but have since lost my attention thanks to the woman standing next to me.

I like that she's softening. Opening up to me a little. I just wish I were more over my own shit to be able to do something about it.

"I have to get out there, but thanks for the coffee."

"Oh, yeah, of course. You're welcome. You're sure me being here won't distract him?"

"Him? No. Me? That's another story."

Her cheeks flush and a small smile plays on her lips. "Don't you have a team to coach?"

"Yep. And nothing would please me more than to show you how good I am."

"At what?"

"Everything." Giving her a quick wink, I turn and jog slowly onto the field.

When practice ends, Bryce runs from the field and straight into his mother's arms. "How'd I do? Are you proud of me?"

Shock is written all over Sadie's face. "Proud of you? I am beyond proud of you. You were amazing out there."

Bryce is beaming, the compliment his mother laid on him filling more inside him than he can possibly comprehend. Elated, Bryce runs back onto the field where a couple of the other boys are still working on a few plays we showed them.

"Everything all right?" I ask Sadie as I begin to pack the gear up.

"Huh? Yeah. Fine. I just..."

"I know it's none of my business. You've made that perfectly clear, but..." I pause, hoping I don't completely destroy the small amount of progress we've made. "His dad is gone. He knows that. It's you he's trying to impress. So, he, uh, so he doesn't lose you, too."

"He would never lose me," Sadie says. I can hear the argument gearing in her voice.

"I know that. And you know that. But his little kid logic doesn't. Trust me."

My words are greeted with silence. Fearing the worst, I begin to explain what I mean, but she cuts me off. "Is that how you felt as a kid? Like you had to work extra hard to keep what you loved?"

"I started by trying to be the best kid I could. Good grades, good behavior. Kicking ass at football. It wasn't until..." I clear my throat. "It was until my mom got sick that I realized the truth."

"Which is?"

"I didn't need to earn anyone's love. Not my mom's. Not my grandmother's. Their love was constant and unconditional. It wasn't me who wasn't good enough, it was him."

"I'm sorry. No child should have to go through that."

"It sucked back then. But now, I realize how great I had it."

Sadie looks away as she speaks. "I just want to protect him, you know?"

"Of course you do. Unfortunately, you can't. Not from everything at least."

"It's not you."

"What isn't?" I ask. I stop what I'm doing and face her.

"I don't hate you."

"Could have fooled me," I say with a laugh.

"I don't. I just... I'm afraid to let anyone in. As a friend or otherwise. I'm afraid of getting attached and being left in the dust again. I'm afraid of getting hurt. Most of all, I'm afraid of Bryce getting caught in the crossfire of it all. I don't want him to get hurt again. I can't bear to see that pain in his eyes."

"I know I can't make any guarantees."

"But?"

"But I have no intention of hurting you or Bryce. Nor do I intend on going anywhere anytime soon. I just want to be friends. Hell, I would settle for getting along. And I'd really like to spend some time with Bryce."

"He adores you."

"I'm pretty fond of him, too." I tuck a strand of hair behind her ear. "You can't keep pushing people away, Sadie. That's no way to live."

Her eyes flutter open and meet mine. "I'll try."

Bryce comes running up to us and I'm so thankful for the disruption before I do something stupid like kiss her. Because that fear and sadness I see in her eyes makes me want to do just that—kiss her, and it, away.

"Can we go get some ice cream?" he asks. "Maybe Billy can come with."

"Oh, well..." Sadie fumbles for words.

My hand ruffles Bryce's hair. "I wish I could, but I have plans."

"A date?" Bryce pries.

I nearly choke on the question. "Why in the world would you ask that?"

"Aunt Jules says all the ladies in town are talking about you and that you're a fine piece of—" Sadie's hand covers Bryce's mouth before he can finish his sentence.

"No way am I dating that guy," I say, pointing to the man stepping out of the vehicle that just parked near us.

"Is that...?"

"The one and only," I tell him. I rest my hand on his shoulder. "Come on, I'll introduce you." Bryce jumps up, throwing his fist in the air. I turn toward Sadie, looking for her permission. "If that's okay with you?"

"It's more than okay."

I lead Bryce and Sadie over to where Mason is standing. "Hey, man, sorry I missed practice."

"Feels like we're back in college," I tease as I pull him in for a hug.

"Ha-ha. Who do we have here?" Mason squats down in front of Bryce.

"I'm Bryce," he says with a confidence he didn't have when he met me. I'm not sure why—if it's because I really am his favorite player or if it's because I'm at his side and that makes it easier somehow. Either option makes me feel pretty special.

"Good to meet you, Bryce," Mason says as he shakes his hand. He slides his sunglasses off as he rises to his feet. "And you are?"

"Sadie," she replies, extending her hand to him. "It's nice to meet you." I look back at her, stunned. "What?"

"He gets greeted like that, but I have to spend weeks trying to earn a non-yelling voice from you?"

Sadie shrugs. "He seems nice."

"I'll show you nice," I say in a teasing tone.

At that moment, Avery emerges from the car. I hadn't even noticed her sitting in there, but I couldn't be happier to see her. "Aves," I say, excitement filling my voice as I wrap my arms around her.

"Easy there, Saint," Mason warns, which only makes me hug her tighter. For a while, moments like this with Avery were exactly what I wanted despite knowing they had feelings for each other. I honestly never thought Mason would act on them, but seeing them now? I couldn't be happier.

Out of the corner of my eye, I catch a glimpse of Sadie, who is back to shifting uncomfortably. I smile, hoping that it's out of pure jealousy. "Avery, this is my neighbor, Sadie, and her son, Bryce."

"It's so nice to meet you," Avery says as she moves in and takes Sadie off guard with a hug.

"Oh. Hi." Sadie wraps her arms around Avery as she gives me a wide-eyed look.

The sight of her and Bryce with my friends only solidifies what I already know. I'm falling. Hard. It's crazy how right this looks. How much I enjoy the picture of my two worlds colliding. How, despite this being a football practice, not once has my pity party started or my downward spiral continued. I found peace. And it's all thanks to that gorgeous brunette who finally doesn't hate me.

"Billy's taking us to dinner tonight. You should join us," I hear Avery suggest. Secretly, I pray Sadie agrees. This moment feels right and I'm not ready for it to end.

"Oh, no. I don't want to impose," Sadie says.

"Impose?" Avery laughs. "You'd be saving me from these two. Really."

"Go, Mom," Bryce urges her. "I can spend the night with Grams. You deserve to have a little fun."

"You just want to go to Grams' house because she feeds you junk food instead of vegetables," Sadie says.

"Duh," Bryce replies.

"I don't know."

"Please? Do it for me?" Avery says, her hands pressed together in the praying position.

Sadie laughs as she gives in to Avery's begging. "Okay, sure. Sounds fun."

We chat a while longer and then Sadie and Bryce take off to get ready for tonight.

"You're welcome," Avery says, looking all too pleased with herself.

"For what exactly?" I ask.

"Getting her to join us? Turning this into a double date?"

"Don't let her hear you say that word. There's a good chance she'd skin me alive. This isn't a date. The woman just started tolerating me. I don't want to screw that up."

"But you do want to screw her?" Mason so eloquently chimes in. Rather than her normal scolding, Avery folds her arms across her chest and awaits my reply as well.

"Fine, yes," I say, throwing my arms in the air in frustration. "But it's not going to happen, so you can stop whatever this is right now."

"She's perfect for you," Avery says as if I don't already know.

"Maybe so, but I'm not going to push her. And hell, let's be honest. I'm still fucked in the head. She doesn't deserve to deal with that."

"You're no more fucked up than the rest of us," Mason says.

Somehow, I'm not so sure.

Chapter 17

Sadie

When I step into Grams' bar, Billy, Avery, and Mason are already there.

Billy had been kind enough to offer me a ride, but I insisted on driving myself just in case I felt it necessary to bolt. What exactly I would need to escape from, I'm not sure. This isn't a big deal. Just a few people having some dinner. In my grandmother's establishment, nonetheless.

I hesitate, staying near the entrance, bracing myself for what the night may hold. I urge myself to relax by reminding myself it's nothing more than a night out with friends. Just because one of those friends sets my body on fire and makes my heart feel like it's going to implode doesn't mean anything. All I have to do is keep my distance. Remain calm. And not let him touch me.

When Billy sees me, he stands from his seat and waves me over.

Still needing a minute to compose myself, I hold up a finger, letting him know I need a second. My feet lead me to the bar where Grams is grabbing a beer for Frank, one of her regulars.

"Hey there, sweetie pie," she greets me. Frank's smile widens. "Not you, you old fool."

"Hey, Grams."

"Uh-oh. What's wrong?"

"Nothing. Why would you ask that?"

"I'm old, but I'm not stupid. I can see the look on your face. You're nervous about something."

I nod in the direction of the table Billy is occupying.

"That sexy neighbor of yours finally make a move?"

"What? No. I'm meeting him and his friends and I'm just a little nervous he might think this is a date or something. Which it isn't. I just... I am so out of practice."

Grams pats my hand. "You're going to be fine. Just try and have some fun. You do remember what that is, don't you?"

"Bryce and I always—"

She shakes her head. "I mean adult fun. Alcohol, laughter... sex."

The mortification from her mentioning the word sex has my nerves settling and my desire to get away from her increasing and sending me straight to the table where Billy sits.

"Glad you could make it," he says, pulling out a chair for me.

"Thanks for inviting me," I reply. There's a nervous twinge in my voice that I pray no one else can hear.

Billy stands and pulls out the chair next to him.

"You're really going all out to prove this nice guy thing, huh?"

"Just sit down," he tells me, followed up with a slight laugh.

I take my seat, the conversation flowing easily between us from the start. I'm loving hearing about their stories from college. The trouble Mason used to get both of them in. I especially love how red Billy's cheeks get, a clear indication of his embarrassment in me hearing these stories.

For as nervous as I was when I arrived, I now feel completely at ease. Even when Billy's arm comes to rest on the back of my chair. Sure, I can feel the heat from it; it's sweltering. I don't shy away, though. He's impossible to resist and if I'm honest, I'm tired of resisting him.

It's just after midnight when Avery yawns. The sound and motion are exaggerated. "I'm exhausted."

"Oh, yeah. We should probably call it a night," I agree.

"No, no, no. You two stay," Avery says. "My handsome husband can see me back to our hotel."

"Hotel?" I ask, sounding surprised.

"Yeah, Mason's a little too ritzy to stay at such a... shithole? Is that the term you used?" Billy says with a laugh.

"Shithole. Death trap. Whatever, I'm not staying there," Mason says. "Night, man. Great to meet you, Sadie."

"You, too. Both of you," I reply just as Avery pulls me in for a hug.

"Don't do anything we wouldn't do," Avery says as she bounces off, her arms wrapped tightly around her husband's waist.

"Sorry about them. They're..."

"Adorable?"

Billy rolls his eyes. "They're something. I'm not sure adorable is the right word. However, I am glad Mase finally pulled his head out of his ass and made a go of things with her."

"Speaking of going... I should probably get going, too."

"Do you have to? It's still pretty early."

"What would people think if they saw us together?" I gasp.

"You're worried about tonight after the display you put on last week? Kissing me like that in front of all these people?"

I know he's teasing, but my cheeks flush at the memory of it. And he seems to be loving the reaction he's instilling in me.

"I... uh... I'm going to get us some drinks."

Before Billy can argue, I run from the table and straight to the bar.

"What's got you all flustered? That handsome hunk at the table, I hope?"

"Not now, Grams. Drinks. I need drinks. Lots of them."

"Coming right up," Grams says.

Tapping my fingers on the bar as I wait for Grams, I see the door to the right of me open. Out of anyone who could have possibly stepped through that door, never in a million years would I have expected to see my ex.

My heart begins to race as I fill with panic. The woman attached to his hip, the gorgeous blonde at least five years younger than me, sends my insecurities through the roof.

My body freezes, my feet cemented to the floor.

What in the hell is he doing here? What the hell am I going to do? What the hell am I going to say?

Completely panicked, I rush back to the table and grab Billy's arm. "I need a favor."

"I thought you were getting drinks," he says.

"Not now. Please. I need you to do something for me. I'll owe you. Big."

"Now we're talking," he teases. His face sobers when he sees I'm not returning his smile. "What is it? What's wrong?"

"I need you to... Oh, God, I can't believe I'm even asking this but..."

"Just tell me and I'll do it."

"I need you to pretend to be my date."

"I'm sorry, what? Why?"

"Please, Billy. I'll explain later. I just really need you to do this for me. I know you have no reason to help me, but—"

"Oh, I have plenty of reason," Billy says, sipping the last of his drink. "I would say lead the way, but looks like you don't have to."

"Billy Saint, I thought that was you," Jon's voice boasts. He extends his hand to Billy, who does nothing more than look at it.

I don't know why it hadn't occurred to me that they might know each other or at least met. Jon knows most of the players in the league or has at least interacted with them on some level. I'm not sure if Billy's displeasure at seeing Jon is due to the fact that he abandoned his son or if they have some sort of history. Whatever it is, I hope it doesn't deter Billy from playing along with this little charade.

"Is there a reason you're here talking to my wife?" Jon asks.

"Ex-wife," Billy corrects him. His arm snakes around me and gives me a squeeze. "And we've done a lot more than just talk."

"Is that so?" Jon laughs. "What is this, some sort of joke?"

"Do I look like I'm laughing?" Billy replies.

"What are you doing here, Jon?" I ask, Billy's body against mine giving me the strength to stand up to him.

"It's Bryce's birthday this week. Why else would I be here?" he asks.

I can't help but feel like it's to torture me. "He'll be thrilled."

"So, what, are you two dating or something? And I use the term dating loosely."

"That's exactly what we're doing. Have a problem with it?"

Jon's gaze falls to me. "You're pathetic, you know that?"

"Excuse me?" My voice is raised and filled with anger. I take a step toward him, Billy's grip holding me from going too far.

"If you're in town to see your son, I suggest you do that and leave Sadie alone," Billy informs him in no uncertain terms.

"She's my wi—"

"Ex-wife," Billy corrects him again.

And while I know the ex belongs there, I'm not quite sure why Jon keeps referring to me as his wife. Present tense. He's the one who left. He's the one who filed for divorce. So why is he trying to take this macho possessive stance over me?

"And you can communicate any visitation with Bryce through me. I don't want you to even think about Sadie, understood?"

"You have no right."

"Take it or leave it. Or else, I'll make you regret you ever stepped foot in this town."

Billy presses his palm to the small of my back and guides me outside, leaving a gaping Jon in his wake.

My fingers fumble in my purse for my keys. When I finally get them out, Billy takes them from my hand and opens the passenger door for me. "Get in."

"I'm okay. I can drive myself. I just... thank you. I..."

"Sadie, if you don't get in the car and make it look like we're leaving together, it's going to make all that in there worthless. He's watching like a hawk. Now, get in."

"What about your car?"

"I'll come grab it tomorrow. Let's go."

I slide into the passenger seat and pull my seat belt over my lap.

A moment later, I burst out laughing.

"Mind telling me what's so funny?" Billy asks.

"Did you see his face when you told him to make arrangements through you? He was speechless."

"You look way too pleased with all this."

"Why shouldn't I be? Look at what he was trying to throw in my face. Some young, hot girl who is probably a model? The one he probably left me for? I know it's childish, but..."

"You wanted payback?"

I nod. "And I dragged you into the middle of it. I'm so sorry."

"Oh, yeah. That was rough. Having to pretend that a gorgeous woman was my girlfriend. Woe is me."

"You know as well as I do how people in this town talk. Before we know it... the whole town will be planning our wedding."

Billy shrugs. "Let them."

"So, you want to marry me?"

A sweet smile covers his face. "I could imagine worse things in life."

"Such as?"

"Being married to your ex's new girlfriend. Mara is high-maintenance to the extreme. He has no idea what he's gotten himself into."

"Do I even want to know how you know that?"

His face remains forward. "Probably not."

Jealousy begins to bubble in me. I'm not sure if it's because he knows Mara intimately. Or because he and Jon seem to have the same taste in women. Whatever it is, it bugs the hell out of me that he knows her. Maybe dated her even.

"It was a long time ago," he continues.

"It's none of my business." Especially since the knowledge does little to ease the raging jealousy in me.

Billy pulls the car in front of my house and kills the engine. "Sadie, look..."

I don't say anything, just step out of the car. He's at my side in an instant. "You can stop now. I doubt he followed us."

"Just to be safe."

Billy walks me to the front door of the house, where I proceed to slide my key into the lock without so much as looking at him. I owe him a thank you. Maybe even an explanation for my abrupt change in behavior. Neither I'm willing to give right now—thanks to Mara.

"Hey, wait." His hand catches my wrist as I move to step inside. "What happened? What did I do?"

"Nothing. I'm just tired."

"Come on, Sadie. We both know that's not true. You were ecstatic moments ago and now you can't seem to get away from me fast enough. Did I do something? Say something?" He pauses as he tries to rack his brain over what could have caused my abrupt mood swing. The look in his eyes implores me to tell him, to let him make right whatever is wrong.

Since I don't quite feel like coming across as some sort of jealous fake girlfriend, I decide to do the opposite. Touching my hand to his cheek, I tell him, "Everything's fine. Really. Thank you for tonight. I'm sorry if I caused you any trouble."

"You're no trouble at all, Sadie," he tells me, his hands dropping to my waist. "In fact, I am more than happy to be your boyfriend— or whatever else you need me to be—when you need it."

His head dips toward mine.

Uh-oh. I'm in so much trouble. He gently brushes his lips against mine.

When the kiss ends, we stand there breathless. His forehead resting against mine. "So good," he murmurs.

Good is an understatement. That kiss was... life-altering.

Brushing his nose against mine, he says, "Good night, baby. I'll see you tomorrow."

Chapter 18

Sadie

T he light of day comes way too soon for the restless night's sleep I had. Between the run-in with Jon and that kiss from Billy, how was a girl supposed to get any rest? I touch my lips, still able to feel Billy there, and find myself wishing he hadn't been a gentleman, that he had kissed me harder—deeper.

Lying in bed with my eyes closed, I envision what it would have been like. What he would have been like. Hard yet thorough. Tender, but rough. The way he touches me, even in the most innocent of ways, has this possessiveness about it. A sexually charged possessiveness that is hot as hell.

The knock on my front door interrupts my thoughts and immediately has me hoping that it's Billy. I jump out of bed and tie my hair up in a knot on top of my head.

"Hey," I say as I pull the door open.

"Hey yourself," Jon says as he pushes his way into my home.

My good mood deflates as I let out a groan of displeasure. With my hand holding the door in place, I take in a deep breath. "What are you doing here?"

"Where's your boyfriend?"

"My what?"

"Oh, so Billy isn't your boyfriend?"

"He is my boyfriend. What I'm still trying to figure out is why you're here."

"Why isn't he?"

I roll my eyes. Where is this coming from? Why is he so concerned about whether or not Billy and I are dating? He. Left. Me. And our son. He has no right to question our lives. Rather than dignify his question, I turn the topic to the reason he told me he was in town. Surely, he isn't here to see me. "Bryce isn't here. He spent the night at his friend Tommy's house."

"And where's Billy?"

"Are you jealous or something?"

Jon scoffs at my comment. "Hardly. He is more than welcome to my—"

Like clockwork, I hear the screen door slam behind me. When Jon's face falls, I know exactly who it is. I turn to face Billy, my eyes pleading with him to just play along. But he's already ahead of me. He steps closer and presses a kiss to the tip of my nose.

"You were out of coffee, so I went to get us some." He hands me a cup from the holder. "Four sugars, all the cream, just the way you like it."

As if the fact that he walked into this situation seamlessly and played along isn't enough. The fact that he knows my coffee order? That just blows my mind. And makes my heart skip a beat.

Pushing down the fact that not only are we playing this game, but my heart is trying to weasel its way in, I smile up at Billy. "Thanks, baby."

I may have never said the words to him before, but it's undeniable how right they feel. And from the looks of it, he thinks so, too.

"This has to be a joke," Jon says, finally chiming in.

"I thought I told you to contact me if you needed to arrange times to see Bryce?" Billy looks around the house. "Clearly, he isn't here. You shouldn't be either." He takes a sip of his coffee as his arm comes to rest over my shoulders.

"Clearly. Seems Sadie can't be bothered to be a mother now that her new fuck boy is around."

My heart breaks at the dig. Regardless of what he thinks of me as a woman, I would have hoped he knew what a good mother I am. Or at least how hard I work to be. To hear him say that? Tears instantly well in my eyes, my body trembling. I'm about to give him a piece of my mind, or at least attempt to, when Billy jumps in for me.

"Get the fuck out." Billy's voice is booming and angry. There's an intensity to it that instantly stops the trembling. The shock of Jon's accusation wearing off and becoming replaced with anger.

The cup of coffee falls from Billy's hand and splatters onto the floor as he charges toward Jon. There's no comparison in size. Billy towers over Jon. Even with his injury, I'm certain Jon doesn't stand a chance against him.

"Get out before I remove you."

Billy's hands clench at his sides, a clear indication that he's trying to restrain himself. As much as I would love to see him punch Jon, I'm grateful. Because at the end of the day, Jon is still Bryce's father. And Bryce would be devastated if anything happened to him. And even more if he found out Billy was the one to do it.

Jon backs up, eyes still set on Billy. I can see the trepidation in the way he moves, the quickness in his step. When he reaches the door, he stops and turns back to us. His mouth forms the beginning of a sentence, but before he can speak, Billy shuts him down.

"You want to be pissed that someone is satisfying your ex-wife more than you ever could? Have at it. But be pissed at yourself for giving her up. Take it out on me if you want. I don't give a fuck. But if you ever insult her again? Ever insinuate that she is anything but an amazing and loving mother? I will end you without so much as a lost night's sleep. Man up, be a father, and stay the fuck away from Sadie."

Jon shoves the door open with enough force that the screen door comes off its hinges. He walks down the path and to his car. All this without even a word about wanting to see his son or spend time with him.

I stand here, shell-shocked, confused as hell by what just transpired. I'm not sure whether I should focus on the anger toward Jon, the gratitude toward Billy, or the sadness that seeps into my chest.

"You okay?" Billy asks.

I nod. Unable to speak. Unable to move.

"Do not listen to him. Do not let him get in your head." Billy moves in my direction, his hand caressing my face the same way it did yesterday. "You are an amazing mother. An amazing person. Bryce is lucky to have you."

I know he's trying to help, so I give him a soft smile in return for his kind words.

"Come on, baby. You know you're a great mom. Bryce, he adores you."

"Thank you," I tell him, removing his hands from me. I turn away, unable to look at him. "It's not just that. It's all of it."

"All of what?"

"Jon being back. You. This stupid lie. Christ, Billy, I am so sorry I dragged you into this."

I can hear him laugh behind me. "You didn't drag me into anything."

"Stop doing that."

"Doing what?"

"Acting like this isn't a big deal. Twice now, in less than twenty-four hours, you've pretended to be my boyfriend."

"And?"

"You did it because—"

Billy's thumb runs across my bottom lip. "I did it for you. For Bryce. To make that dickhead suffer for leaving his wife and son. You didn't make me do anything, Sadie. I did it because I wanted to."

"What about Faith?"

Billy's eyes widen. "What about her?"

"I overheard her talking about you and—"

"There is nothing going on between me and Faith. Or me and Tara. Or, hell, me and anyone for that matter." A sly grin crosses his face. "Well, except for you."

Had my jealousy really been that obvious?

"Why... I... How?"

"You're not as difficult to read as you'd like to think. And believe me, Sadie. I spend a lot of time *reading* you."

My cheeks flush instantly.

"If there is anyone in this world I would want to date, it's you." My mouth falls lax at his admission. "Thing is, I'm not in the right headspace to date anyone right now. Believe me, I wish I were, but I'm just not." His knuckles gently slide across my cheek. "I want to do this. I want to help you. I want to know what it's like to be with you. Even if it is only pretend."

"You would want to date... me?"

I watch his eyes roam my body slowly. They scour every inch, first down, then back up until we're eye to eye again. "Damn right I would."

I shake my head, unable to believe that this god of a man, someone who can and has had everyone they've ever wanted, would actually want little old me. "And if we were dating. What would you want to do right now?"

The question is dangerous. Being with him like this makes me want to live dangerously. It makes me want to be the girl I used to be. The one who seized life and enjoyed every minute of it.

His jaw ticks, his gaze hardening. "You know what I want, Sadie. All I need is for you to give me permission to do what I've been wanting to do since the moment I laid eyes on you."

"Kiss me," I murmur.

A smile slowly creeps onto his face. "Just a kiss? I need to know, Sadie. I need to know so I don't push too far. Because once I kiss you? I won't want to stop. And if all you want is a kiss, I'm going to need to control myself."

Holy shitballs. "Um..."

His lips gently brush against mine. "What's it going to be, Sadie?"

"Take whatever you want." I gasp, realizing what I just said. What it is that I agreed to.

His head dips slowly, lips a whisper from mine.

"Hey, Mom," Bryce's voice calls out. "What happened to the door?"

Billy jumps back and stumbles over the table, falling back onto the couch. Bryce looks at him curiously. "You okay, Coach Billy?"

"Yeah, bud. Sure am. You, uh, you just scared me."

Bryce's eyes see the spilled cup of coffee on the floor, then glances back at the door. "Did someone break in?"

"No, honey, nothing like that." I wrap my arms around him. "Billy was nice enough to bring me some coffee this morning and the wind took the door and broke it."

"Yeah," Billy agrees. "And then, while we were talking, I dropped my coffee. At least I never did that with the football, right?"

"Thank you," I mouth to Billy. Bryce doesn't even notice the quick wink Billy shoots my way.

"Can I help you work on the house today?" Bryce asks Billy.

"Bryce, you can't keep—"

"Of course," Billy says at the same time. "Go upstairs and grab your stuff, then meet me outside."

At the sound of Billy's invitation, Bryce bolts up the stairs. I should be angry that he didn't check with me first, but all I can think about is him kissing me.

Billy watches Bryce dash up the stairs with a smile on his face. The minute he's out of sight, Billy steps over the now broken table and stands before me.

"I'll replace that," he says. "Now, where were we?"

"Billy..." I say, pressing a hand to his chest. It doesn't deter him, though. And the moment his lips meet mine, I am so grateful that it didn't.

The kiss is short-lived, but even so, it makes my toes curl.

Billy pulls away, his forehead resting against mine, and chuckles. "I love Bryce, but the kid has shit timing."

Hearing him say that he loves my son instills a whole bunch of emotion in me that I don't want to consider.

"You need to go," I say, pushing him toward the door.

"What? Why?"

"Thank you for letting Bryce help you today. I'll come get him in a couple of hours so that he doesn't take up your entire day."

"He can stay as long as he likes. Sadie, talk to me. What did I do?"

Bryce comes down the stairs. "Ready."

"Have fun, guys." I press a kiss to the top of Bryce's head and go to the kitchen.

Chapter 19

Billy

I swing the hammer against the wall. The sound of it breaking through the drywall is cathartic.

Coming to New Hope was supposed to be a peaceful and calming experience for me. Something to help me get back on my feet. So far, it's been anything but.

It all started the moment I laid eyes on Sadie. Sassy, sexy Sadie. The woman took me by surprise. Not just how damn beautiful she is, but how damn drawn to her I am. She's done nothing but push me away, yet I can't get enough. She makes me feel alive again when for so long I felt numb inside. And just when I thought we were making progress, her ex shows up.

Jon Hart. Football reporter extraordinaire. The guy I introduced Mara to when I needed to get her off my back. If Sadie finds out, there is no way in hell she's not going to blame me for her marriage ending. I can already see it now.

For whatever reason, Jon didn't leak my secret. He doesn't owe me anything. Quite the opposite actually. Not long before I came to New Hope, Jon has approached me, begged me for an exclusive tell all interview. Tara thought it was a great idea too, so I agreed—at first. The more I thought about it, the more I realized I couldn't go through with it and I ended up backing out. He was furious. So why is he doing this? Why is he keeping my secret? Why not tell Sadie the truth?

I look over to where Bryce is painting the trim I have laid out on the sawhorses. I smile, watching him work so intently, much the way he does at practice. As I watch him, I catch a glimpse of him looking back at me. I wonder if he's looking for my approval. Trying to impress me. It's something I did often myself as a kid. The moment I completed a chore or did something that my mom or grandmother didn't ask me to do, I would run to them and tell them what I had done, seeking their praise and approval. And hoping it was enough to keep them around.

After all, I hadn't done that with my father, and he left. Maybe had I shown him what a good boy I could be, he would have stuck around. That's what I thought as a kid. Now, I know better. I sure as hell don't want Bryce feeling like that.

Walking over to him, I set my hand on his shoulder. "Great job, kid."

"Thanks, Billy," he says eagerly. "I'm trying really hard."

"I can tell." I pause a moment. "You know, when I first came here, I thought this was going to be a temporary place for me. A nice project to work on and then I would head back home."

As expected, Bryce's face falls.

"And now..."

He lifts his eyes to meet mine.

"Now I don't think I could imagine living anywhere else."

"Really?"

"Really."

"Is it because Mom doesn't hate you anymore?"

Turning my head in the direction of Sadie's house, I smile when I see her watching us from the porch. "Yeah, it is."

I know I told Sadie I was in no place for a relationship, but...

I'm hoping that by fixing up this place, I can fix myself, too. Repair some of the damaged pieces of me to become someone worthy of Sadie. And Bryce.

The sound of a loud car horn comes blaring down the street.

I know I'm not Bryce's father. I have no right to, well, anything really. Still, despite the excitement I see on his face, my hands hold his shoulders and keep him in place.

"I knew it," Bryce shouts. "I knew he would come."

He busts out of my grip and runs toward the car.

"Hey, Champ," Jon greets him when he steps from the vehicle, Mara stepping out after.

"Dad, I knew you would make it. Mom told me not to get my hopes up, but I knew you wouldn't pass up a football party."

Jon pulls Bryce in for a hug but never confirms that he'll be attending the party.

I make my way over to where Sadie's standing.

"He's not staying," she says. "I don't know what the hell is going on, but he's not here for Bryce."

That's when it dawns on me. He's here for me. But why? I'm nothing more than a washed-up, injured football player. My body tenses at the revelation.

"Hey, what is it?" Sadie asks.

"He's here for me," I whisper. "I just don't know why." As if I didn't feel guilty enough knowing that I inadvertently ended his parents' marriage, now Jon's using his son to get to me.

Bryce is talking a mile a minute and Jon finally seems to be paying attention. Or, at least, he's pretending to. As long as Bryce is none the wiser, I don't care which it is.

"So, what do you think about your mom dating a famous football player?" Jon asks Bryce.

"Dating? Like boyfriend and girlfriend?" Bryce's eyes widen. "That's so cool."

Sadie's next to me, shaking her head in disbelief. Her little white lie just got a whole lot bigger. And a whole lot more dangerous.

"Bryce, go inside." Sadie's words come out an order.

"But—"

"Inside, now."

Bryce does as he's told, leaving the three of us squaring off again like we did last night, with Mara standing off to the side, clueless as always.

"How dare you?" Sadie shouts at Jon.

Jon holds his hands up innocently. The fucker is far from innocent. "I didn't do anything. I figured he would know that the two of you are so in love."

"After what you did to him, do you think I'm going to tell him about every man who enters my life? No way in hell would I put him through that." She throws her hands up in disbelief. I can see the guilt and anger in her eyes, and I hate that he put them there.

Sure, she's the one who came up with the lie, but he's the one who brought his kid into it.

"We didn't want to tell Bryce until we knew for sure where this is going. We didn't want to get his hopes up," I say through gritted teeth.

"Looks like the cat's out of the bag now. I mean, what's the big deal? He survived our divorce. I'm sure he'll be fine when you two break up." Jon laughs.

I'm not sure if Jon is underestimating the effect his actions had on his son, or if he just doesn't care. It's hard to gauge.

"Survived," Sadie shouts. "Survived? He barely survived it. But you wouldn't know that because you weren't around. You weren't the one who spent night after night holding him until he cried himself to sleep. You wouldn't know any of what Bryce went through when you left because you couldn't even be bothered to pick up the damn phone."

"I didn't answer because I didn't want to hear you begging me to come back again." Jon says the words proudly.

"I only begged for the sake of our family. For our son." Sadie's body is shaking with anger. "If you came to spend time with Bryce, then I suggest you do that. If you came here for any other reason, then just get the fuck out."

Jon rolls his eyes as if the idea of him being here for any other reason than his son is preposterous. "I'm here to spend time with my son. And introduce him to my fiancée."

Mara wiggles her fingers at Sadie. If Jon was looking for a reaction from Sadie, she sure as hell isn't giving him one. She stands before him, unaffected by his announcement.

"Then do it," Sadie tells him. "Let Bryce know I'll be at Billy's and to come get me if he needs anything."

As though it's the most natural thing in the world, Sadie turns and makes her way into my home. When I join her, she's already on the couch, knees to her chest and tears streaming down her face.

At the sight, I rush to her side. "Sadie, it's going to be okay. We'll figure this out."

"I can't let Bryce think we're together. He's already too attached to you. It's going to destroy him when you leave."

"Leave? I'm not going anywhere, Sadie."

"My God. What have I done? I'm just as bad as him playing this stupid game. One look at Mara and I immediately felt inferior. I get why he left me now. She's fucking gorgeous. All I wanted was to show him that someone might want me too. Let him see what it feels like to be replaced with someone better. All this just to make myself feel better. And at what cost? Bryce."

"Sadie..."

"Don't. Don't try and defend me. There is something wrong with me."

"There is absolutely nothing wrong with you." I pause for a moment. "Listen, I know this seems bad."

"Seems?"

"Yes, seems. But there's an easy solution." She remains silent, the look in her eyes urging me to continue. "We go on a date."

"A date? What does that solve?"

"It means we continue our little charade." I can feel her ready to protest. "Hear me out. We give Jon the payback he deserves, while figuring out what the hell he's actually doing in town."

"What about Bryce?"

"Is there really any harm in him thinking we're dating?"

"Um, yeah. When Jon leaves town and it ends, he'll be devastated."

"Not if we're still friends." I shrug. "Just because we break up doesn't mean we have to hate each other. Things just go back to the way they used to be."

"I used to hate you," she reminds me, a hint of a smile playing on her lips.

"Well, we both know you had shitty taste in men. Thankfully, that's improved," I say as I press my finger to my chest.

"I wouldn't go that far," she says. There is the slightest of smiles on her face. "I don't know, Billy. This all sounds so complicated. I think it's best if I just come clean to Jon. I'll die of embarrassment, but it will be short-lived since there's no way he'll be sticking around for long."

"And how is Bryce going to take that?"

Sadie drops her head in her hands. "This is such a mess."

"Really, it's not. My plan is perfect. Flawless even. And we get the best of both worlds."

"How do you figure?"

"Well, the way I see it, I get to date the hottest girl in town while pissing off her douche of an ex-husband. Maybe I even get to kiss her a few times—you know, for authenticity. And when all is said and done, I get to keep her as a friend."

Sadie groans before raising her head, eyes meeting mine. "I don't know."

I shake my head. "You deserve to have payback. And you deserve a man who's going to treat you well."

"And you're that man?"

"Damn right I am. If you don't believe me, I have references."

"I bet you do."

"Go out with me tonight, Sadie. Let's show that asshole what he's missing out on. Let's show him what it is he can't have anymore. What do you have to lose?"

"Ugh, fine."

"Not the response I'm used to getting, but I'll take it. Go, check on Bryce and be ready at seven."

"What should I wear?" she asks as I lead her to the door.

"Preferably, nothing."

"Billy."

"Sadie." I say her name with sarcasm and get a swat to my arm for doing so. "You're a gorgeous woman, Sadie. You'll look amazing in whatever you wear." Gently, I press a kiss to her forehead before giving her a slight shove out the door. "Off with you. I have a date to plan."

As she walks back toward her house, she glances back at me and shakes her head.

Chapter 20

Sadie

Thankfully, Jon didn't stay much longer after I returned home. Apparently, he and Mara have "plans" tonight. I may have mentioned that Billy and I do as well, which made him all that much more curious. Not about who was watching Bryce, or anything that really mattered outside of where Billy was taking me. I smiled at him and told him it was a surprise. That Billy always gives me the most wonderful surprises. I left it at that and as soon as Jon was out the door, I rushed over to Bryce to try and explain the whole Billy and me dating thing.

While Jon may be prancing Mara around in Bryce's face, I have never done something like that with a man. Who am I kidding, there haven't been any men for me to do it with. There has been no one since Jon left which is all the more concerning. How would all of this affect Bryce? How would Bryce react to me moving on? Would he be okay with having another man in his life? Especially if that man is Billy. Yet, as I stood before him awaiting his response to my explanation all he did was smile. The more I pressed, the more okay he seemed with all of it. As long as Billy and I keep any kissing to ourselves. His words, not mine.

With one of my fears eased, I stand in the mirror giving myself a once-over which allows a whole other set of them to take over. While he didn't come right out and admit it, something happened between him and Mara. And probably him and Tara, even if it isn't happening right now. My mind wanders down a rabbit hole of the movie star quality women he's left in his wake. And the millions that would pine for a man who not only looked as good as him, but was kind, too. Am I enough for him?

"Get out here already," Jules yells from the living room.

I step out of the bathroom and stand before her. She eyes me from head to toe, taking everything in. Then she twirls her finger in the air so that I show her the full picture. As requested, I twirl around for Jules.

"Damn, girl, you look amazing. You are going to blow that hunky football player's mind—and hopefully something else."

I slap her arm. "Jules."

"What? Like you haven't thought about it? Wanted it?"

"It's not a real date. It's a—" The words stop at the sight of my handsome neighbor standing in the doorway.

Thankfully, he ignores whatever it is that he may have overheard. "Wow."

The single word elicits more out of me than any other compliment I have ever received. This man, a man who could seemingly have any woman he wants, is looking at me as though I am the only woman in the universe.

"Keep looking at me like that and Jon won't have an issue believing we're real anymore," I tell him jokingly.

"The way I am looking at you doesn't have a damn thing to do with your ex."

It's not so much what he says, but the way he says it that leaves me feeling like a jumbled mess. My heart skips a beat, maybe two. My palms begin to sweat. And I can't take the intense pressure the weight of his stare is putting on me. He's looking at me as though I'm some sort of goddess he needs to revere, when I'm just a single mom with stretch marks.

"We should go so we can get this over with," I say, trying to play off the moment and secretly hoping he didn't hear much of my conversation with Jules.

I attempt to move past him, but he grabs my arm. "I'm not trying to get this over with. I'm looking forward to this." He pushes open the door. "Shall we?"

"Hey, Billy," Jules calls from inside the house.

He turns and looks at her, his eyebrows raised in question. "Just in case you were wondering, she's not wearing anything under that dress."

I can feel his body tense next to me. "Thanks for the tip."

"Have fun," Jules calls out as I die of embarrassment with Billy's hand still on my lower back.

He opens the door to his SUV for me and I slide into the passenger seat. His eyes scrape over me and he lets out a low whistle before closing the door and getting in on the driver's side.

I clear my throat of the lump that formed from the looks he's giving me. "So, what's the plan?"

"You'll see."

"Were you able to find out where Jon and Mara were headed tonight?" I ask.

After all, the whole point of tonight is to solidify the lie we've spun.

"Yep."

"Are you going to clue me in?"

He looks at me with a mischievous smile. "Nope."

"Of course you aren't." My voice is filled with frustration.

He chuckles. "Not a fan of surprises?"

"What gave it away?"

A moment later, the SUV slows to a stop across the street from McClaire's. It's an upscale restaurant on the outskirts of town. The exact kind of restaurant Jon would never have taken me to. Unable to handle any more of his gentlemanly gestures, I get out of the vehicle without his assistance and meet him at the front of the car.

"This is where he's taking her?" I hate that it bothers me, but it does. He's giving her everything and I got nothing. That's not true. I did get the only good thing the man had to offer. I got Bryce.

Billy shrugs. "I guess."

He extends his arm out, his hand gesturing to the park behind me. "What are you doing?"

"Taking you on our date."

"That's the park." Before I can continue, string lights illuminate through the park. There's a table set up in the gazebo that's off to the right and soft music plays through the speakers.

"What's all this?"

"A date. Our date." He's standing behind me, his broad chest resting against my back, his hands gently gripping my hips.

"Billy, you didn't have to go to all this trouble. Jon—"

"Like I said, this isn't about Jon."

He has said that. Several times. The problem is, I don't know what it is all about then. Because this is so unexpected. So romantic. So... confusing.

"Do you want to eat first? Or maybe go for a walk?"

He's rattling off suggestions while I am still trying to wrap my head around what's happening. "So, then what is it about?"

"You. Us. Fun."

"You said you're not in the right place for a relationship," I tell him.

"Yeah, I did say that."

"Then all this is just to what? Get me in bed?"

"So, what'll it be? Food or walk?" he asks, completely ignoring my statement.

"Billy," I scold him.

"Food or walk?" he repeats.

"You're unbelievable."

"Now, that I like to hear. So?"

"Walk," I reply.

He extends his arm to me, and I take it, looping mine through his. As we walk through the park, I'm amazed at how much he put into this. Not just the dinner or the music. But the walking path is lit in soft lights as well. My favorite flowers scattered throughout the park. It's perfect.

"I can't believe you did all this."

"Why not? You work so hard between your job, Bryce, putting up with that irritating neighbor of yours. You deserve something nice, Sadie."

"So do you, Billy. More than a slightly bitter, very divorced, single mom with stretch marks."

"Show me."

"Show you what?"

"These stupid stretch marks you keep talking about."

"Absolutely not." He glances around the park, then reaches for my waist. "Stop it."

Swatting his hand away, his fingers skim against the bare skin at my waist, tickling me as they do. A giggle escapes me before I can stop it, immediately upgrading us to a playful push and pull that only results with me in his arms.

"You're beautiful, Sadie, and despite all the hell you've given me since I came to town, I like you."

"I know I'm going to regret this, but..." A small smile plays on Billy's lips as he awaits my words with anticipation. "I like you, too."

"Yeah?"

"Yeah."

The flicker of excitement in his eyes has me tingling. He's going to kiss me; I can see it on his face. He takes a pause, though, giving me the time and space to decline if I want to. Only, I don't. I want him to kiss me.

Just when I think he's going to, he takes my hand and drags me away. "What are you doing?"

Billy comes to a stop, twirling me around until my back hits a tree. "I'm taking this somewhere a little more private."

"Isn't the whole point of this to be seen?"

"Not anymore."

Billy's lips cover mine, his hard body pressing against mine. His hands slide down my arms, around my back, and down to my ass. He squeezes the flesh and I moan into the kiss. His fingers dip beneath the fabric of my dress and the moment he realizes Jules wasn't lying, he emits this guttural growl.

"You're incredible," he tells me when he breaks the kiss.

"Then why are you stopping?"

He brushes his nose along my neck. "Believe me, baby, I don't want to. But, uh, here in the park—not the best place for what I want to do to you."

As if he can sense me becoming unsure of myself, he grinds his hardness against me. "Never doubt how much I want you, baby. Only you."

Unable to formulate a coherent thought, I nod.

"How about dinner?" he asks.

"Will there be dessert?" I stutter out the question.

With his hand on the small of my back, he guides me to the gazebo where are meal is set up. "That's up to you."

He gives me a playful swat on my ass before pulling out my chair.

Billy takes his seat across from me, heat in his eyes. "Quite a beginning to our date."

"I've definitely never had a date that started quite so well before," I say with a smile.

Out of nowhere, a server appears, setting a glass of water in front of Billy and pouring a glass of wine for me.

"Are you sure it doesn't bother you?" I ask before taking a sip.

He shakes his head. "Not at all. Like I said, I went through a pretty rough patch after finding out I wouldn't be able to play again. For whatever reason, I turned to alcohol. It had never been an issue before then, but I'm not willing to risk it, so I just avoid it."

I set down the glass of wine and pick up the water.

"Sadie, really..."

"You told me before that our kisses and anything you might want to do to me would be better if I were sober." I hold up the glass of water. "I'm going to make you prove it."

"Happy to oblige," he says, clinking his glass against mine.

The food is served and as delicious as it is, I find myself more engrossed in our conversation than the food. I think he feels the same way. For two people whose vast majority of conversations consisted of arguments, it seems to be the complete opposite now. We're talking, laughing, sharing old stories. There's a level of comfort with him I never would have anticipated.

When we're done eating, Billy pulls out my chair and gives me his hand to help me to my feet.

"Bryce is at home with Grams," I tell him. "But we could continue this at your place."

"Are you sure?"

"More than sure."

Billy takes my hand and laces my fingers through his.

"Thank you for tonight. It's been wonderful."

So wonderful, in fact, that I had completely forgotten about Jon and the fact that he and Mara were dining right across the street from us. Until I hear his voice bellowing, that is.

"What the hell is this? Are you spying on us?"

With his arm possessively around me, Billy smirks. "It's a date. A romantic one. Not that you would know anything about that." Billy turns to Mara, who's standing off to the side, glaring at Jon. "How was dinner, Mara?"

Her gaze drops to the ground.

Jon is undeterred. "Quite a fall you've taken, Saint. First the knee injury, then the arrest. Now you're hiding out in a small town trying to bang your friend's wife?"

"First off, I'm not hiding. Second, I don't recall us being friends," Billy spits out.

"What are you doing here, Billy? Really."

"I don't know what it is you're expecting to find, but there's nothing there, I assure you. Well, nothing but me, Sadie, and an end to a date I can't wait for."

"Is this some sort of attempt at payback? I take your girl, you take mine?"

The confirmation that Billy and Mara were together makes my stomach feel unsettled.

"That's it. I'm done." Billy steps away from me and directly up to Jon. "I've tried to be nice. I know you're up to something. I don't know what it is, but I'll figure it out. And when I do, I will end you."

Billy ushers me to the SUV and away from Jon.

"Not exactly how I planned for our night to end."

"It's fine."

"No, it isn't. I'll make it up to you. I promise."

"It's probably best if you don't."

"Sadie..."

"I'm sorry, Billy. I just... I think it's better if we just keep our dating pretend."

Hurt and disappointment flashes across his face. "What about our friendship?"

I take his hand and give it a squeeze. "I'd like to keep that if I can."

He brings my hands to his lips and presses a kiss to my knuckles. "Always."

Chapter 21

Sadie

B ryce steps out of the car, his eyes searching the stands. Jon is
nowhere to be found. I curse under my breath, then urge Bryce
to go join his team.

Billy beams down at Bryce, his smile fading when he sees Bryce is
upset. Billy's eyes scan the crowd before finding mine, looking for
the confirmation of what he already knows is true.

He whispers something to Bryce, who then trots onto the field
with the other boys, before making his way to me. "I'm so sorry,
Sadie. This is all my fault."

"How is this your fault?" I ask, confused by his statement.

"The other night. Dinner. I shouldn't have..." He stands before
me with his hands on his hips, his head shaking. "I should have
stayed out of it. Then maybe he would be here."

"Jon hasn't been around for Bryce in over a year. If he's not here
today, it's on him. Not you." My hand tenderly touches his cheek,
tilting his face up until he meets my eyes. "You're the best thing
that's happened to Bryce in a long time." I pull an envelope out of
my purse and hand it to him. "I know Bryce already invited you, but
I wanted to give you an official invitation. Just like the rest of our
friends got."

Billy smiles at me, though the smile doesn't quite meet his eyes
like it usually does. He takes the envelope from me, our fingers
brushing against each other's. "Can't wait." Billy nods in the
direction of the field. "Better get to coaching. I'll see you later."

As I sit in the stands watching the game, I can't help but think
what a mess I've made of things lately. First with Bryce and the

whole not being able to play a game he loves and is really good at because of my own hang-ups. And now, Billy.

"Go Bryce," a loud, cheery voice says next to me.

"You're late," I tell her.

"Yeah, well, at least I'm here, unlike some people. Did that snake of an ex of yours slink back off into whatever hole he crawled out of?" she asks, handing me one of the cups of coffee in her hand.

"I don't think so. But he sure as hell isn't here."

"But Billy is. He's the kind of guy who sticks around. A one-woman kind of guy."

"And how do you know that?" I pry.

"Because it's just who he is. All through high school he and Faith were it. He adored her. She... is Faith."

"Enough said." I laugh. My eyes widen as I watch Bryce raise his arm, the football in his hands. Moving to the edge of my seat, I feel like I'm on pins and needles as I wait for the play to unfold. The ball leaves his hand, sailing through the air in the perfect spiral. I grip Jules's hand next to me when Tommy, on the other side of the field, catches it.

Jules and I jump from our seats, cheering wildly and loudly. As proud as I am of my son, I can't help but notice the excitement Billy expresses as the play concludes. Where he's patted each of the kids on their helmets for a job well done, with Bryce, he swoops him into his arms and spins him around.

"He would make a great dad for Bryce," Jules says when she catches me tearing up at the sight.

There isn't a doubt in my mind that he would. He has such a big heart. "I don't disagree. I just... I can't."

Jules groans in frustration.

"I'm sorry. I know how much you were hoping."

"Sade, honey, I just want you to be happy. Even though you were angrier than shit with him, you were also the most alive and happy I've seen you in a long time. Don't let Jon ruin that for you. Give Billy a chance."

"That's just it. Billy doesn't want a chance."

"Lies."

"I don't mean it like that. I just... he said he's not in the headspace to have a relationship right now. And with everything he's been through, I get it."

"Sadie, he's looked back here at you every thirty seconds or so. Whether he wants to admit it or not, he's there."

I smile when I catch Billy doing exactly as Jules says and stealing a glance at me.

"Maybe we'll get there. Maybe we won't."

His cheeks flush when he realizes he's been caught.

"We're good just like we are right now."

Jules shrugs. "If you say so. Then continue to fake it until you make it."

When the final whistle blows, I leap out of my seat and run to the field. "You did so great," I say to Bryce as I pull him into an embrace.

"Mom, you're embarrassing me," he whines.

As much as I don't want to, I let him go. "Sorry. I'm just so proud of you."

"Thanks. Can we go out for ice cream? A bunch of the team is going."

"Yeah, of course."

Bryce runs back to the boys to celebrate, and I make my way to their super sexy coach.

"Nice game, Coach."

The corner of his mouth tilts up slightly. "Thanks."

"We're going to get some ice cream. Will you join us?"

"I don't think that's a good idea."

"Why not?"

He doesn't answer my question.

"Does this have something to do with the ridiculous blame you're putting on yourself because of Jon not showing?"

"I just don't want to create more problems. I can still"—he lowers his voice—"pretend to be your boyfriend. That's as far as it should go."

"I see." I tap my finger to my chin. "So, you don't think that not coming for ice cream with us isn't going to create more problems? Like breaking Bryce's heart. Not to mention the rest of the team. And maybe even mine."

His head whips up. His eyes looking at me intently.

"I want you to come with us." My fingers run along the lines on his bicep. I bat my eyelashes at him. "Please, Billy? It would make me so, so happy."

"You're not playing fair," he says, swallowing hard.

"What fun is that?" I throw him a look over my shoulder as I walk away.

He scrambles to gather the gear together and slings it over his shoulder before following me. He's hot on my heels in less than a minute.

"You're going to pay for this, Sadie." There's a sexy, mischievous glint in his eyes.

"Dearly, I hope."

"You're killing me here." He groans.

Chapter 22

Billy

I settle myself onto the chair on the back deck. As much as I would love to start working right now, no way am I ready to endure the wrath of my very sexy and stubborn neighbor. Not after the progress we made.

Perhaps we had a bit of a setback at dinner the other night, one that's had her keeping me at arm's length since. At least I'm still in her good graces. She smiles at me rather than yells. She allows me to spend time with Bryce, which is my priority since his own father can't be bothered even though he's back in town.

Why is he back, though?

Why now?

Considering he's spent little to no time with his son, I doubt it's because of a sudden pang of guilt for abandoning his family. No, if my instincts are right, he's back because of me. He's a journalist after all and journalists dig. I'm just not quite sure what it is he's hoping to unearth on me. I don't have any secrets. And this thing with Sadie is amazing, but certainly not newsworthy.

When I realized Jon was Sadie's ex, my heart sank. As thrilled as I was to play her pretend boyfriend, playing this game with him is dangerous. Not that I seem to be keeping anything under control with it. For fuck's sake, I've almost attacked the guy more than once. Still, if Sadie finds out I introduced Jon to Mara, she'll never speak to me again. Losing her is the last thing I want. Since Sadie walked into my life, hell on wheels as she was, I've felt more like myself. I've felt alive again.

Even though I told her I didn't think I could handle having a relationship with anyone right now, I can't handle not having one with her. This little game of pretend we're playing is fine—for now. There is absolutely nothing pretend about us. Not for me at least. I want the woman and I don't stand a chance in hell of denying it.

Sadie has consumed my mind from the moment I stepped foot in this town. I thought this house was going to give me a purpose. Help me move past the past and into the future. Little did I know that it wasn't the house so much as the woman living next door to it that would make all the difference.

In the peaceful early morning, I close my eyes and focus on the sounds of nature. Only it isn't just the birds I hear chirping. My eyes fly open at what sounds like sobbing. Glancing over toward Sadie's house, I see her sitting on the swing, her knees to her chest.

I make my way over, the creaking of the gate as I open it causing her eyes to fly up to meet mine.

"Billy?"

"You okay?"

"Yeah, I'm fine. Sorry."

I may be an uninvited guest, but she isn't pushing me away either. When I reach the back porch, I make my way to her swing. "Mind if I sit?"

She doesn't speak but shakes her head. Her face is tear-stained. Her eyes red and puffy. The moment I'm next to her, she falls apart. Her head rests on my chest, the tears staining my shirt.

"What is it, Sadie? What's wrong? Is it Bryce?"

She shakes her head again.

"Did Jon do something?" I ask, anger rising inside me. I can already feel the urge to pounce and yet I have no idea what it is he did.

"No, nothing like that," she assures me. "It's, uh..."

The sobs overcome her again. All I want is to make whatever it is that's troubling her better, but I don't know how.

"Talk to me, Sadie. Let me help."

"You can't." She says that but has no clue about the lengths I would go just to make her smile.

"I'll do anything, Sadie. And I mean anything." I tilt her chin up so she's forced to look me in the eye. "What is it, baby?"

"Jack. He's gone."

My heart sinks, knowing the pain she's going through. The little boy she wasn't supposed to bond with but couldn't help but to because he reminded her of her own son at home.

"I'm so sorry, baby. He was a great kid."

Sobs rack through her body again, this time even worse than before. It's as though saying the words broke a damn she didn't even know was there. My arms hold her tightly as her head drops to my chest. We sit, just like that, for a long time. Not long enough, though. Not for me. I would be more than happy to never let her go and spend the rest of my life with her in my arms.

I think of the little boy I met. The one I know she bonded with more than she should have. How could you not, though? The kid was amazing, full of life despite the shitty hand he had been dealt.

She brushes away the tears. "I keep trying to remind myself that he's gone to a better place and that he's no longer in pain, but..."

I don't speak, only hold her tighter as I let her work through her thoughts and emotions. She's right. I can't make this better for her. All I can do is be here and be whatever it is that she needs me to be in this moment. Her neighbor that she hates, the guy who's becoming her friend, the fake boyfriend, or the man I wish I were— a man who's hers. Whatever it is, whatever she needs, I'll deliver.

"He didn't deserve this. He had his whole life ahead of him and now it's just... gone. He didn't get to enjoy anything."

My hand smooths over her hair. "You're right. He didn't. None of those kids you take care of do. Just because he didn't get to live a long life doesn't mean he didn't get to lead a good one." Sadie looks up at me as though I've lost my mind. How in the world could I possibly say that an innocent little boy who suffered from repeat brain tumors his entire life had a good life? "He had parents who loved him. Tons of friends. And, he had you. You make every one of those kids' lives better, Sadie. Jack knew you loved him."

Wiping away the tears, Sadie turns her head and gazes up at me. "Thank you."

She brushes her lips against mine, soft and sweet. The last thing I want is to say the words I need to say, but I have to. As much as I would love for this to escalate and turn into something more, it can't.

"Sadie..." I groan.

"I need you, Billy. I need you to make me feel good again. There's just been so much and you—you're the only good thing I have right now, besides Bryce. I just... please, I need you." Sadie situates herself onto my lap, straddling me. Her hands hold my face near hers, eyes boring into mine.

Fucking hell, I might be a bastard right now, but there is no way in hell I can resist when she presses her mouth to mine again, her tongue sliding across the seam of my lips, begging for entry. I fall so damn far from who I am and what I should be doing because this woman just annihilated me. I grip her hips, pulling her further against me, deepening the kiss as I do.

"You sure about this? You let me keep kissing you, I might not stop."

"Don't. Don't stop, Billy."

I swallow hard, resisting the urge to just take her right this minute. "Are you saying what I think you're saying?"

"Yes."

Our lips meet in a searing kiss. I reach for the hem of her shirt and pull it over her head. My eyes land on her breasts in the lace and lick my lips. She reaches for my shirt, her hands seemingly desperate to touch me. Who am I to deny her anything? Her hands slide under my shirt running along my skin until she's able to slide the material over my head. The moment it's gone, our lips crash together again. Just as desperate for her, I run my fingers over her silky skin, up her arms until I loop my fingers through her bra strap. I grip the straps of her bra and yank it down with a firmness that causes her breasts to spill out. As I take her in, admiring every inch of her, she undoes her bra and tosses it to the side.

Her nipples peak against the hard planes of my body. My fingers dance at the elastic band of her scrub pants. "Do you want me to touch you, Sadie? Do you want me to fuck you with my fingers?"

"Yes."

"Yes, what?" I growl, low and deep, into her ear. I can feel her thighs clench around me.

"Yes. F-fuck me, Billy."

My teeth gently sink into the skin at the nape of her neck as my fingers find their way to her hot, soaked center. "Is this what you want, Sadie?"

When she moans the word "yes" I slide my finger inside her, curling it just right to hit her G-spot.

"Oh, God." She looks sexy as hell, her head falling back, her tits arching up to me.

"You like that, baby? You want more?"

"Yes. Please. Please, Billy."

The sound of her begging has my lips curving into a smile. She rocks against my hand, her pussy begging for more. Something I am more than willing to give her. When I withdraw my finger, she whimpers.

"Billy." My name is a plea on her lips.

Trying to sate the need in her, I flick my tongue over her nipple.

"More," she pants out.

My mouth closes around her nipple, sucking it and teasing it until she curses. I can feel her body begin to tense, the tension building inside of her. Replacing the single finger that I removed with two this time, her body jolts. She grips my shoulders, nails sinking into my skin. Unabashedly, Sadie begins to rise and lower herself onto my fingers, taking what she needs from me.

"Come for me, Sadie."

She pushes herself further onto my fingers, sinking them further into her and grinding roughly against them. I can feel her walls clench around them, her head falling back in ecstasy. Her body is racked with pleasured shudders as she rides out her orgasm.

Her head drops to my shoulder as she comes down from her high.

"Better?" I ask.

"Much," she replies.

Her eyes lock with mine and I'm afraid of what it might mean. I realize I'm so wrapped up in my own bliss that I've completely forgotten about him. "Billy. I'm so sorry."

"Sorry? For what? That was the sexiest thing I have ever seen," I tell her as my fingers run up and down her back.

I feel her hand reaching for the hardness that sits between us, the realization of her concern finally dawning on me. I smile up at her. "It's okay, Sadie. I'm perfectly content just like this."

"Why are you so good to me?"

"You might not like the answer if I tell you."

She presses her lips to mine in a chaste kiss. "You might be surprised."

"Another day, Sadie. Today, just let me be here for you."

She nods and rests her head against my shoulder again. I'm not sure how long we sit like this, but we remain in the same position until I hear Bryce's voice calling out through the house. Sadie hears

it, too and scrambles off my lap and into the seat next to me. I toss
her shirt to her. She manages to slide it over her head just as Bryce
walks out the door. Bryce looks at us suspiciously when he makes his
way onto the back porch, Jules following behind.

"Hey, Mom. Hey, Billy." Bryce pauses. "Are you two doing that
gross kissing thing?"

"Billy was just trying to make me feel better," she tells him. "I had
a pretty rough day at work."

Jules stands behind Bryce, holding Sadie's bra in the air and
quirking an eyebrow up at us. Sadie is glaring at Jules. Something
Bryce notices instantly. He turns to look at Jules, who flings the bra
into the bushes.

All I can do is sit here and shake my head as I chew on my cheek
to stop the laughter from erupting.

Bryce shrugs, gives Jules a hug goodbye, and heads back into the
house.

"I am so proud of you," Jules squeals.

"That's my cue to leave," I announce as I stand from the swing.

"Why, stud? Don't you want to hear what Sadie has to say about
whatever just happened between you two?"

Before departing I press a kiss to the top of Sadie's head. "If you
need me, I'm here."

Jules's demeanor changes instantly. "Sade, what is it? What's
wrong?"

As I walk away, I hear a whole new set of sobs taking over Sadie. It
takes everything in me to not turn around and give her a million
more orgasms, so she never feels bad again.

Chapter 23

Billy

It's been three days since me and Sadie had our moment on her back porch. Since then, nothing. She's essentially blown off every attempt I make. Today, though, she can't run.

Today is Bryce's birthday party.

Today is the day I put this game to an end and make this official.

"You made it," Billy shouts as I enter the backyard where his birthday party is already in full swing.

Sadie really outdid herself, especially considering she isn't a fan of football. From the football decorations to the mini football field that she spray painted in the grass.

"Wouldn't miss it for the world," I tell him, accepting the embrace he gives me. "Happy Birthday, buddy."

Sadie walks over with a smile. "Hi, Billy."

"Hey, Sadie."

"I'm glad you're here."

"Me, too."

"We need to talk," Sadie tells me.

About time. "Yeah, of course."

"Mom, can Billy come play football with me and the guys before you do your weird adult stuff?"

I shrug. "He is the birthday boy."

"Of course. Just... find me when you get a chance?"

"Find you? I never take my eyes off you," I tell her. Before I can gauge the expression on Sadie's face, Bryce grabs my hand and leads me farther into the party where the kids are tossing a football around.

As much as I want to talk to Sadie, I'm having a blast with Bryce and the other kids. This is what it's about. Making a difference. Teaching young kids to become athletes. Giving people something good to focus their energy on rather than drugs, or gangs, or worse.

The kids seem to be enjoying themselves, too. Admittedly, they've improved over the past couple weeks. Especially Bryce. How could he not, though, when he spends every waking hour playing, perfecting? Much better than the stupid iPad Sadie said he had been glued to for months.

Out of the corner of my eye, I glimpse Jon and Mara. I watch as they make their way over to Sadie, Jon putting on quite the production and doing everything he can to rub Mara in her face.

At least that's why I think he's doing. I'm not quite sure yet. I have Mason looking into a few things for me, but so far, he's come up empty-handed.

Sadie seems to be taking the confrontation in stride, but I can see it eating at her on the inside. An unobservant dick like Jon would never notice, though. He's so wrapped up in whatever game he's playing, he would never notice what's going on with anyone else. Hell, he hasn't even come to wish his own kid a happy birthday.

I hear someone yell "heads up" and when I turn around, a ball is flying at me. My hands jut out instantly and grip the pigskin. The kids ooh and aah when I catch it, then begin to vie for it. I toss the ball up in the air and watch as they scramble for it.

When I glance back a moment later, Sadie's gone, but Jon is still standing there, his head thrown back and laughing. My eyes scan the small crowd for Sadie, hoping she merely moved on to mingle, but she's nowhere to be found. She must have gone into the house to escape Jon. As I contemplate going after her and risking her wrath, a football hits me square in the chest with a thud.

"Jesus, Tommy, nice throw," I say as I rub the spot where the ball hit. I gently toss it to Bryce. "I'll be back in a minute."

The kids immediately go back to playing as I head off in search of Sadie.

I don't have to look far. One step into the kitchen and my eyes fall on her standing at the sink, her fingers gripping the edge and her head hanging down.

"Hey," I greet her, joining her in the kitchen.

She slowly takes a breath in and blows it out. "Hi."

"Anything I can do to help?"

She shakes her head.

I approach her cautiously. She's already upset and things between us these past few days have been more tense than usual, so I want to give her some space. But the moment I'm near her, she turns to me and wraps her arms around my waist. Her head rests on my chest and I can feel the soft sobs that are taking over her.

"Shh," I coo as I stroke her hair. "It's going to be okay."

"Am I ever going to quit feeling like this?"

"Like what?"

"Like I'm a failure? Like I'm not good enough?"

"Sadie..."

"Why wasn't I enough? Why weren't we enough?"

I cup her face in my hands and force her to look me in the eyes. "You're enough, baby. You're more than enough. It's him who isn't."

"I'm not in love with him. Hell, I don't even like him. It's just..."

"Something you put your heart and soul into was ripped away from you unexpectedly and you don't have a clue as to what you did to deserve it?"

The corner of her mouth curls up. "Who knew two very different situations could be so similar?"

Standing there silently, we gaze into each other's eyes. Words are left unspoken, but the sentiment and emotion are still there.

"Thank you, Billy."

"Nothing to thank me for."

"I disagree."

"Of course you do," I tease.

"Oh, shut up." Sadie playfully pushes on my chest, as if I'm going to let her go that easily.

"Make me."

"Okay."

"Okay? What the hell—"

Her lips press to mine in a searing kiss. The gentle hold I had her in tightens, my hands reaching for the flesh beneath the back of her shirt. Skin like silk glides under my hands as I press her to me, deepening the kiss.

When we finally pull apart, we're both breathless and taken aback. I rest my forehead against hers. "You can make me shut up anytime."

"Like now?"

"Why, Sadie, do I reckon that you might like kissing me?"

Her fingers hook through the belt loops on my jeans. "Damn right I do."

"Whoa, baby." Jules's voice breaks through the haze we're in, ending this moment that Sadie and I are having. "I wish someone would kiss me like that."

"What do you want, Jules?" Sadie asks, her voice filled with frustration.

"The birthday boy is requesting cake. Probably just so he can get to his presents. Or present, because I'm pretty sure he's only interested in what Mr. Football Player over here got him."

Sadie looks up at me suspiciously. "What did you do?"

"Nothing, I swear," I say, raising my hands in innocence.

"He doesn't need to be spoiled," Sadie argues.

While I wholeheartedly agree, I don't consider the gift I got him spoiling. "My grandmother wouldn't call it spoiling. She would say he was just very loved."

"You're trouble."

I sling my arm over her shoulders. "Pot meet kettle. Now, where's that cake?" I rub my hands together as I glance around the kitchen. Jules pulls it from the fridge and hands it to me.

"Put those muscles to use," she tells me.

Sneaking a peek, I see the football-shaped cake inside the box. "Great job, Mom. He's going to love it."

"Just take the cake outside," she orders me.

"Enjoy the view on my way out," I tell them, but the words are intended for Sadie. With a little sway of my hips, I carry the cake out to the table that's set up for the cake.

Bryce runs over, and Sadie and Jules step up to the table as well. Bryce's eyes light up when he sees the cake. "This is so cool. Thanks, Mom."

For the first time all afternoon, Sadie looks at peace. I should have known it would take something as simple as a smile from her son to do that. Even with Jon across the table from us, Sadie eases into the moment and begins to belt out "Happy Birthday."

Bryce hurries through his slice of cake and waits anxiously to open his gifts.

"Mine first," Jon boasts proudly. He waves Bryce over to the oversized box wrapped in red paper.

Bryce tears at the paper, thanking his dad before even knowing what's inside.

"Well, what do you think?" Jon asks. He flashes Sadie a smug smile as he proudly stands next to his gift.

"A bike?" Bryce asks.

"Yeah, it's the one you wanted," Jon says, seeming impressed with himself that he remembered something about his son. "Why aren't you more excited?"

"I am. It's just..."

Jon looks at his son, clueless. Bryce turns to Sadie for help.

"He already has a bike. This bike. He got it for his birthday. Last year."

"It's okay, Dad. Now I have two. In case one gets a flat tire," Bryce says, trying to make his dad feel better.

"How about another gift?" Sadie suggests. She grabs a box off the table and hands it to him.

"It's from Billy," Bryce says.

"You can open that later," I say. I may hate the guy, but I sure as shit don't want to upstage him in front of his son.

"Nonsense, he'll open it now," Sadie says, returning to her place next to me. We stand close, my hand resting on her back. To most, we look like the happy couple we're supposed to. To Bryce, our interaction could be taken as merely friendly. Exactly what we want him to continue to think.

"Sadie, I, uh... I may have—"

"Loved Bryce too much?" She laughs. "At least someone does."

She smiles happily as he opens the gift, the game console he had been wanting inside.

"Oh my God, this is so awesome. And look, it even has a football game with it," Bryce shouts as he shows his friends.

"Of course it does," Sadie says. Her eyes find mine. "It's too much..." she says. I begin to protest, but she holds up a hand to stop me. "But thank you."

"You're not mad?"

She looks back at Bryce. "How can I be when he's smiling like that?"

The kids are all huddled around him; he's beaming from ear to ear. And then, he's on his feet. He runs toward me at top speed, his body slamming into mine as his arms engulf me in an embrace. "Thank you. Thank you. Thank you."

"You're welcome, man. Now, quit worrying about the game and focus on the field for me, okay?"

"Was this your way of making me work harder?" he asks. I reply with a shrug. "I will. I promise."

"Smooth," Sadie says as we stand there watching Bryce run back to his friends.

"What can I say? I was sick of hearing about it during practice. Now that he has one, maybe he'll shut up and become the awesome quarterback I know he can be."

"Quarterback, huh? Not a defensive end like his favorite player?"

"He's got too good of an arm for that. Plus"—I kick my leg out —"the quarterbacks are the ones that are protected. It's guys like me who do the protecting. Figured you would prefer him in a safe position."

"So thoughtful."

"What the hell do you think you're doing?" Jon shouts as he approaches Sadie and me.

Instinctually, my arms come around her and move her behind me in order to protect her.

"Not the time or place, man," I tell him, though I doubt he's going to listen.

"He's my son," Jon reminds me.

I resist the urge to laugh and keep my comments to myself. "Just let it go."

I'm walking a fine line between wanting to kick his ass—not only for walking away from his family, but for continuously trying to make Sadie doubt her self-worth. The guy is a prick and if he weren't Bryce's father, I would have shown him already what happens to guys like him.

Jon places his hands on my chest and shoves me. I stumble back slightly, my knee giving way. Regaining my balance, I straighten and look him in the eye. "Don't do this. Not here, not today."

"Fuck you, Saint. This is my family. That's my son. You're not wanted here."

"Dad, don't. Billy's my friend," Bryce says, running toward his dad.

"Billy is using you to get to your mom." Jon spits out the vile accusation and Bryce instantly looks dejected.

"That's not true, B. You know me better than that. But I think it's best if I go. I'll see you at practice tomorrow," I tell Bryce. He looks confused and uncertain, and all I want to do is hug him and tell him his father is a liar. But I bite my tongue. It's best for Bryce if I just leave before this gets any worse.

Bryce nods.

"Go, enjoy your party. I'll see you tomorrow."

Slowly, Bryce makes his way back to his friends, his head turning and looking back in our direction every few steps.

"You have a lot of nerve," Sadie growls under her breath at Jon.

"Don't. It's not worth it. Today is about Bryce and—"

"And Bryce wants you here," she assures me.

"And I want to be here. But I won't ruin his day. Not for anything."

I press a kiss to Sadie's forehead and head for the gate.

I'm almost to my porch when I hear Sadie call out my name. I stop and turn. She's jogging toward me, then stops when she reaches my stairs. "I'm so sorry about that."

"You have nothing to be sorry for."

"You didn't have to leave."

"As much as I hate that he won that round, no way in hell was I going to let Bryce witness any of it. Especially not today."

"Thank you for thinking of my son before yourself. Thank you for, well... everything."

"My pleasure."

"The party ends in an hour. Bryce and I have a silly little tradition of watching an old movie and eating way too much popcorn. Would you want to join us?"

"I appreciate the offer, but I don't want to impose on your tradition."

"Bryce would love for you to join us." She pauses for a moment. "So would I."

"When you put it that way..."

Sadie moves up a step as I move down one. I'm towering over her, but when I dip my head, I'm able to press my lips firmly to hers.

"I guess I'll see you in an hour then," I say.

Sadie heads down the steps and back toward the yard. As I watch her walk away, I notice a little more pep in her step and a sexy smile plastered on her face every time she looks back at me.

Finding the woman sexy was one thing.

This falling in love with her bit is a whole other.

Chapter 24

Sadie

"**M**om, why do you look so nervous?" Bryce asks as he watches me flit across the living room.

"What do you mean? I'm not nervous. I just want to tidy up a bit before we watch the movie."

There's a knock at the door and I damn near jump out of my skin.

"I'll get it," Bryce shouts as he leaps up from his seat.

I didn't mention that Billy was joining us just in case something fell through. Or I chickened out, which I damn near did. Now, with him standing in my living room, there's no way out.

"Billy's here," Bryce announces cheerfully as if anyone could miss the hulking football player with how much space he takes up in my home. And, if I'm honest, my mind.

"Glad you could join us." I try to say the words casually, but even I can hear the nervousness in it.

The playful smile on his lips tells me that he hears it, too.

"I'll go grab the movie," Bryce says as he bounds up the stairs at top speed.

"Having second thoughts?" Billy asks as he slowly makes his way to me. I shake my head in response, the scent of his cologne taking over my senses and rendering me speechless. The man smells as good as he looks.

He brushes his thumb over my bottom lip. "I want to kiss you again, Sadie."

"I want that, too."

Just as he's about to, just as the one thing I've been thinking of nonstop since we kissed on his porch is about to happen, I hear Bryce's footsteps on the stairs.

"Got it." Bryce walks into the living room, holding up the case. "Have you seen this movie before, Billy?"

"*The Sandlot*? I have. It's a great movie."

"Mom says it's a classic."

"That it is." Billy leans down and whispers into my ear, "As in we're old enough to be classics."

"Speak for yourself," I say, bouncing my hip slightly against his.

Bryce jumps onto the center couch cushion. He pulls the bowl of popcorn into his lap and pats the seat next to him. "Sit here, Billy."

Billy does as instructed and once we're settled, I turn on the movie. While it might be a classic and one of my all-time favorites, I'm having a hard time watching it instead of the man on the opposite end of the couch. Out of the corner of my eye, I see Billy grab a handful of popcorn from the bowl. He pops a few in his mouth and then, without looking, tosses a piece at me.

"Hey," I scold him.

His eyes are glued to the television, but there's an evil smile on his face. He takes another piece and throws it at Bryce this time.

Bryce stares wide-eyed at Billy, then looks back at me.

"Oh, it's on," I say, reaching for a handful of popcorn and throwing some at Billy.

Before I know it, popcorn is flying everywhere, Bryce is laughing hysterically, and the movie is long forgotten.

Out of ammunition, I reach for a pillow.

"Oh no, you don't," Billy says, lunging for me. His arms wrap around my waist and before I know it, I'm off the ground.

"Put me down," I say with a giggle.

"Drop the pillow." Billy's words are a playful order.

"What makes you think I was going to use it on you?"

"Call it a hunch," he says.

"I'll save you, Mom," Bryce says as he grabs another pillow and strikes Billy in the back with it.

Pretending as though the hit from the eight-year-old boy was enough to knock a grown man down, Billy falls onto the couch, taking me with him. We land with a thud, my body on top of his. Bryce piles on a moment later.

"That was so much fun," he squeals with excitement. "Can that be a new part of our tradition?"

Can it? Will Billy even be around long enough to make his ninth birthday? Would he even want to be?

The question hangs in the air, and I turn my attention back to the movie, only this time Bryce has taken the edge seat, leaving me stuck next to Billy. It's like torture to be so close to something you want so badly but can't have. As all these crazy thoughts roll through my head, I hear the sound of Billy yawning next to me.

I glance over and see his arms stretched out above his head and as they come down, one relaxes on the back of the couch, slowly sliding its way to my shoulder. I bite my bottom lip, trying not to smile at the high school attempt to put his arm around a girl, but appreciate the effort considering Bryce is right next to me. His fingers trace small circles on the bare skin of my arm.

"What are you doing?" I whisper to him.

"Flirting."

"Why?"

"Because that's what you do when you like someone."

I do my best to hide the smile that wants to emerge, but I can't help it. The guy is sweet and smooth and so damn sexy that when I'm with him, I can't help but smile. I allow his arm to remain because the warmth of his body feels too good to turn away.

Bryce is fast asleep by the time the movie ends. There's so much reverence in the way Billy looks at Bryce, as if he can't imagine these moments with him are real. For all the fear of Billy leaving us, I'm starting to think that it would tear him about just as much as it would us.

"I need to get him up to bed," I say. I begin to move off the couch, but Billy sets his hand on my leg.

"Let me."

"You don't—"

"I want to."

Effortlessly, Billy scoops up Bryce into his arms and makes his way up the stairs. The entire time, I can't take my eyes off them. The visual is picture-perfect. Something straight out of a Hallmark movie, so beautiful that I actually tear up.

I swat the tears away and do my best to compose myself when I hear Billy's heavy footsteps on the stairs. He's making his way back down and I'm not sure what play he's going to make, but I want to be prepared for anything.

When he reaches the bottom, he stops. "It's getting late. I should probably go."

"Oh, yeah, right," I say, scrambling off the couch. Of all the things I expected to happen, him offering to leave was not one of them.

"Unless..."

"No, it's fine." I make my way to the door. The moment my hand touches the handle, I feel Billy's hands gripping my waist.

"I want to stay, Sadie. I just want to know that you want me, too. I don't want to assume anything or push you. It's been a tough day for you."

"It was. But it's better now." I rest my head against his strong chest. I shouldn't be doing this. I should be letting him leave—making him leave—because falling in love isn't an option for me. Not until Bryce is grown, at least.

"Well, I'm glad. Is there something I can do to make it even better?"

"This is pretty good right here."

"What about this?" His hand slides under my shirt, his fingers dancing along the skin of my stomach.

"That's nice, too."

He presses his lips to my neck, and I let out a slight moan. My thighs clench, my panties dampen, and my hands grip onto the denim material at his thighs.

"You're so responsive."

"You're so good." My cheeks flush and I'm not sure if it's because of my admission or the feeling of the finger that slipped beneath the waistband of my jeans.

"Tell me what you want, Sadie. Tell me what you need."

"I want... I need..."

"Mom?"

"Yeah?" I call out.

"My tummy hurts."

I groan, thinking of all the cake and candy he consumed today.

"Coming," I tell him. "I'm sorry," I say to Billy, who doesn't seem the slightest bit upset by the interruption.

"To be continued," he says softly before pressing a final kiss to my cheek and heading out the door. I close the door behind him and rest against it and sigh.

"Is Billy still here?"

"No, honey. He just left."

"I didn't get to thank him."

"You can thank him tomorrow."

After giving Bryce his medicine, I slide into the bed next to him and wrap him in my arms.

Chapter 25

Billy

So close.

Yet so far away.

I need to figure out a way to get Sadie alone. Just for a night.

As much as I love hanging out with Bryce, right now I need a little more of his mom, too. Ever since she rode my fingers, taking whatever she could from me to get herself off, I spend an exponential amount of time wondering what else I could do to make her come. I've already conjured up a long list. Now I just want to put it to use.

Something shifted the night of Bryce's party. I'm not sure what it was or how it happened, but I could feel it. So could Sadie. That's why our little popcorn fight resulted in us almost making love.

I grab my phone, a plan suddenly generating in my head.

"This is Jules."

"Hey, Jules, I need a favor."

"Does said favor result in Sadie having a good time? And by good time I mean—"

"I know what you mean," I say, hoping to halt her from continuing her sentence. "And... yes. It does. Hopefully."

"This is Sadie. Hopefully is all we can... hope for? Oye. I need to work on my vocabulary. So, what's the favor?"

"Can you take Bryce for the night? I want to cook Sadie dinner and..."

"Fuck her?"

I shake my head. "There's that sparkling personality. So, what do you say?"

Jules goes silent, pretending as though she wants to think about it when I'm fairly certain her sole purpose in life right now is getting Sadie laid.

"Under one condition."

I roll my eyes. This should be good. "And that is?" There's another long pause. This time I don't think it's pretend, though. I think she's really hesitating. "Just spit it out, Jules."

"Never mind. I'll watch Bryce tonight. No issue."

"You're sure?" I have a feeling whatever it was that she was going to ask had to do with Travis.

"Positive. Be at her place at seven. Oh, and, stud?"

"Yeah?"

"Don't forget the protection."

"Goodbye, Jules."

***

Seven sharp, I stand on Sadie's doorstep. No flowers. No pretense. Because I don't want to scare her off thinking this is a date. Which it is. I will let her get to that conclusion on her own when she sees what I've cooked up for her. Literally.

"Hey," she says as she pulls open the door. She looks me up and down and smiles. "What's up?"

"Are you busy?" I ask.

"Jules is here. Why? Everything okay?" She peeks around me. "Is Jon up to something?"

I shake my head. "No. I was hoping you would have dinner with me tonight."

"That's so sweet. I would love to, but like I said, Jules is here and —"

"And she came to hang out with Bryce," Jules tells Sadie with a smile.

"Why do I feel like I'm being set up?"

"Clearly, you're paranoid," I tell her.

Jules hands a small bag to Sadie, then gives her a slight shove out the door. "You two kids have fun. Only do things I would do."

Sadie cringes at the sound of the door slamming behind her.

A moment later, her eyes, filled with questions, flash up and meet mine. "What are you up to?"

Extending my hand to her, she places hers in it. "You'll see."

We walk in the direction of my house, but when I turn toward the front porch, she stops. "What are you doing? I thought we were going out to dinner?"

"I never said we were going out."

She hesitates for a moment, standing at the bottom of the steps. "What's with you luring people into your house?"

"Are you coming or not?"

She steps gingerly through the door and into the house. "You know, the last time you were here, you just barged in. Actually, every time you've been here, you just barged in."

"First off, I didn't barge in. I entered with implied permission."

Raising an eyebrow at her, I encourage her to continue.

"I thought my son was in danger."

"Don't be so dramatic. And that still doesn't explain the day you barged in at six in the morning with nothing but some tiny shorts and a tank top that was dangerously tight."

"Dangerously?" She half laughs, half squeaks.

"Yep. Dangerous for my sanity."

I lead her through the kitchen to the back deck. One of the few things in this place I don't have to fix.

She emits a small gasp when she steps outside. "Billy. This is beautiful. Did you do this for me?"

"Nah. I like my deck to look like a garden that's about to go up in flames," I tease regarding the mass quantities of flowers and candles scattered all over.

"What is all this for?"

I pull out the chair at the table and nod for her to sit. "I'm capable of more than you know. And I did it because, well, you've had a shit few weeks and deserve to have someone take care of you. Plus, I've heard putting up with that asshole neighbor of yours isn't easy."

Watching a woman blush has never been a turn-on of mine. But in this case, it's sexy as hell. "Eh, neighbor guy isn't so bad. I may have misjudged him. A little."

"Only a little, huh?"

"It seems that maybe I didn't know him as well as I thought I did."

"I hear he's an open book. Willing to answer any question you throw at him."

"Why did you come back here?"

"Straight shooter. I like that. Well, to be honest, I felt lost after I had to give up football. It's my life—was my life. And I'm not really sure what to do or where to go from here."

Sadie nods in understanding. "I get it. Different reason, but same feeling. That's exactly how I felt after my divorce. Lost. Alone. Unsure. So, I came here to where I knew I would be safe. With Grams."

"I guess I kind of came back for the same reason. My grandmother is gone," I say, leaning against the post. "But it's home. And I need a little of what that home feeling brings you. However, I hadn't realized just how far home had fallen."

"Bit off more than you can chew?"

"Understatement of the year," I say with a chuckle. "I'm more than capable of paying someone to do the work for me. I just need to do it myself."

"I get that."

"Hungry?" The question comes out of left field and is a dead giveaway on his need to change the subject.

"Starving."

"Great, I'll get the food ready."

"I don't want food."

Chapter 26

Sadie

B illy stops dead in his tracks, his jaw damn near hitting the floor at my unexpected comment. "Then... what do you want?"

Throwing caution into the wind, I move from the chair and walk over to him. I reach up and touch his face. He remains silent, standing there, letting me do whatever I want without complaint. Before I can chicken out, I lift onto my toes and press my lips against his.

It's as though this kiss unhinged him. Billy grabs my waist and pulls me to him. What began with me being in control has resulted in him taking over. Skilled lips, strong arms, and a gentle touch knock my senses for a loop.

"God, I love kissing you," he tells me, his lips leaving mine and nipping at my ear.

"Then kiss me, Billy," I say. It's not a whisper or a suggestion. It's a demand. "And don't stop.

He blinks his eyes, confusion filling them. Maybe disbelief. And when he flashes them open again, there's excitement. "Are you sure about his?"

"Positive."

The moment he has confirmation, the gloves come off. I'm in his arms and over his shoulder and being taken into the house caveman style. And I'm laughing. Giggling, really, the entire way. He drops me onto the bed and the soft mattress feels amazing beneath me.

Billy grabs the bottom of his shirt and pulls it over his head, discarding it on the floor. I'm the one in disbelief now. The man is unreal. Toned perfection.

He rakes his eyes over me as though he's formulating a plan of attack—where he's going to kiss first. What position he's going to take me in.

"Strip for me, Sadie."

The intense gaze in his eyes sets off a myriad of emotions in me. Fear, nervousness, unworthiness. "I can't."

"It wasn't a question, baby. Do it before I lose my patience."

I slide down the bed until my feet touch the floor. I stand before him as I work the buttons on my jeans. I swallow down my fear as I shove them over my hips and down to the floor.

"Now your shirt."

I close my eyes, trying to remember that I've already been shirtless before him. Everyone looks better in the moonlight, though, right? Now, here under the lights, I hesitate. Billy clears his throat, his eyes set on mine. Pulling the T-shirt over my head, I let it fall from my hand and hit the floor next to me. Unclasping my bra, I drop it next to the shirt.

"Come here."

I do as Billy asks and slowly walk toward him.

It can't be comfortable, but he's down on his knees before me. He loops his fingers into the material of my panties. Then slowly lowers them down my legs. I'm standing before him, completely naked, light filtering in. His fingers trace over the scar on my lower abdomen before he presses his lips to the same spot.

"You are fucking gorgeous. The most beautiful woman I have ever seen."

I run my fingers through his hair. He remembered and he doesn't care. Just like he said he wouldn't.

"I want you, Sadie. I want to make love to you. I want to claim you."

"I-I want that, too," I pant out the words.

"Lie on the bed. Spread your legs."

I do as Billy instructs me to. Lying here naked as he stands over me, I feel completely exposed, yet utterly adored.

"You're wet."

I nod.

He kneels between my thighs and presses a kiss to my lips. He trails the kisses from my lips to my jawline, then down my neck. My body trembles under his touch, gentle yet commanding. I'm like putty in his hands. Everything about him makes me lose my head. I'm lost in him and the sensations his hands and mouth leave on my body.

He closes his mouth around my nipple. I lift my head, watching him suck and nip at the sensitive area. There's something so sexy, erotic even, about watching him pleasure me. I arch up, my hands gripping the sheets as he sets every square inch of my body on fire. His fingers tickle my skin as they slide down my body to my core. He runs his fingers through the wetness at my core, then brings them to his lips, tasting me on his fingers.

"So good."

"Oh, God. Please, Billy."

"Please, Billy, what?"

"Taste me, Billy. Fuck me with your mouth."

A wicked smile crosses his sweet face. His mouth covers my center, his tongue flicking over my swollen bud as a finger teases my opening. Billy grips my hips and angles me up until I feel his tongue penetrating my pussy, then lapping its way back to my clit. He repeats the motion again before slamming two fingers inside me. I cry out, the pleasure and the pain hitting me simultaneously, edging me to the verge of orgasm. The unforgiving pace of his fingers driving inside me pushes me over the edge, my pussy clenching and pulsing until the most intense orgasm I've ever experienced washes over me.

"Oh, Billy, yes." I scream out the words, the pleasure he made me feel filling the room.

He kisses his way back up my body as I come down from my high. "I need you, Sadie. Is this still what you want?"

My hand releases the sheet and wraps around his hard shaft. "What do you think?" I ask as I stroke him.

"Oh, fuck," he growls. He swats my hand away as he sheaths himself in the condom he grabbed from the nightstand.

With his cock in his hand, he lines himself up at my entrance. With one swift motion, Billy moves into me, filling me to the hilt.

"Christ, you feel amazing." He groans as he slides out, then thrusts back in again.

The weight of his body on mine, the physical and emotional connection. It's all there. It's all perfect. And his kiss. His lips moving against mine masterfully as he moves in and out of me.

Nothing has ever felt so good, so real. My eyes flutter shut as I allow each pleasure filled motion to take over me.

"Open your eyes, Sadie." Billy drives deep into me, hips grinding against me, cock pushing me and stretching me.

My eyes open at his request. When I obey, he dips his hand between us, his thumb claiming my clit. Our eyes lock, the passion in his making me reach an unexpected high, and I fall further and further into an orgasmic oblivion, pants, moans, and expletives falling uncontrollably from my lips.

"Holy fuck." The more he watches, the faster he moves. We're a frenzied mess, moving and grinding, seeking out an escape we are both desperate for.

"God, Sadie, yes."

His body trembles as his orgasm hits, his hips bucking into me a few more times before he rolls onto the bed next to me.

"That was... phenomenal." He rolls onto his side, resting his head in his hand. "You are phenomenal."

Embarrassment flushes the skin on my cheeks. I can feel the heat radiating off of them.

"Anyone ever tell you that you're sexy when you blush?"

"Am I? Or is it just because it's you who's caused all this in me?"

"And what exactly did I cause, Nurse Sadie?"

"Tachycardia, a little myocarditis, and pure ecstasy."

He chuckles as he lies next to me, his fingers tracing lazy circles on my exposed belly.

I swat his hand away. "You made your point."

"Not trying to make a point. Just trying to learn your body."

"Oh, so this is research?" I ask as I watch his fingers trace over my skin.

"Mmm. The best kind of research."

He intertwines his fingers with mine as his lips replace his fingers on my body.

"You are... ohhh." He licks my nipple, then blows softly.

He guides my hand, pressing it to his hard dick.

"Already?"

"When it comes to you? Always." His lips slam against mine. The kiss, hard at first, slowly shifts to something more tender. "I've never wanted anyone the way I want you, Sadie."

"Then take me, Billy. Take whatever you want from me."

He smiles down at me. "You have no idea what you just got yourself into."

Hours later, we make our way back to the deck. To the dinner and dessert Billy prepared for us. Billy steps out onto the deck, a beer in each hand. He hands one to me and I take it with a smile.

"Beautiful night," he says as he takes a seat next to me on the swing. The weight of his body causes it to shift, rocking back further than I anticipate.

"Yeah, it is," I say dreamily as I pull the blanket around me tighter. It's not the night I'm talking about as much as the man. A man that not too long ago I hated. A man that turned my body and my world upside down tonight.

My head rests on his shoulder, his head resting atop mine. It's a simple, natural motion. As if we've always been like this. And there, in my heart, starts to seep in the emotion that tells me I want to be like this—forever. For a moment, I allowed myself to forget that this isn't real. Him being here isn't permanent.

"Stay with me tonight," Billy says, pressing a kiss into my hair.

"I shouldn't."

He holds me a little tighter. "You definitely should."

I shift away from him and walk over to the deck railing, the blanket wrapped around my still naked body. "How long do you plan on staying?"

"Where's that coming from?" Billy asks.

"It's always been there, Billy. It's part of the reason I fought this for so long. I knew…"

"Knew what?"

"That you weren't going to stay."

"You knew that, huh? When I don't even know myself?" Silence falls over us. "When I decided to come back to New Hope, I came with one notion—to find a purpose. Then I found you and well, you threw a wrench into my plans. My purpose changed."

"That doesn't answer the question."

"I don't have an answer to your question. A month. A year. Forever. I haven't really given it any thought."

"And it's all I've thought about. When you were leaving. What you leaving would do to me. To Bryce."

"Oh, Christ, baby." He presses his front to my back, his strong arms wrapping around me. "I would never leave you and Bryce. I just found you guys. I don't want to lose you. Besides, I'm not even sure you actually like me yet. I can't give up now."

I falter slightly at his joke. "Maybe we should just go to bed. We can talk about this another time."

"I'm not brushing this under the rug, Sadie. It's why I wanted to see you tonight. To figure out once and for all what was between us. I had hoped earlier was a good sign. Was I wrong?"

"No, you weren't wrong."

Billy presses a kiss to the top of my head, then takes my hand and leads me back into the house, into his room, and straight to his bed. As we lie there, his arms around me. He's holding me so tight that I don't think he'll ever let go. It's then that I realize I don't want him to.

Chapter 27

Sadie

"Well, well, well, look what the cat dragged in," Grams says the moment I step foot into the bar.

"Hi to you, too," I say as I take a seat across from her. She sets a beer in front of me, but I wave it off. "Thanks, Gram, but I'll just have water."

"The look on your face tells me you need something a little bit stronger."

She's not wrong. Right now, though, I need a clear head. "What I need is your advice."

"Bartender advice or grandmother advice?" Grams asks, a teasing smile on her face.

"Grandmother."

She nods. "Make this thing with Billy real. Grab onto that man and don't let go."

"What...? How...?"

Grams scoffs at my confusion. "Oh, please. I can see it a million miles away. The man has had a thing for you since he came to town. And you have been pushing him away since you met him, which tells me that you like him." Grams rests her elbows on the top of the bar and leans toward me. "Quit being so damn scared, Sadie. That isn't like you."

"It's not me I'm worried about."

"Like hell it isn't. I know you don't want Bryce to get hurt either, but you're just as afraid for yourself. For your heart."

"So, what if I am? Is that so terrible?"

"Not terrible, no. But it is debilitating." She takes my hands in hers. "Sadie, sweetie, I know Jon hurt you. And I know what he did to Bryce. But shutting yourself off from anyone else because you're afraid to get hurt isn't fair. Not to Bryce and not to you. What happened to the girl who took chances? To the teenager who sought out the thrill?"

"She became a mom."

"She is still a woman, though. And she still has a heart and needs of her own. Life's too short, Sadie girl. You should know that better than anyone."

The reminder of my parents, their lives cut too short, hits home a little more than I expect. "I know. And I want to. I want to live. And I want Billy. And—"

"He wants you, too," a deep voice says from behind me.

Grams squeezes my hand and excuses herself.

I don't move, fear cementing me to my seat. "Is this some sort of set up?"

"No. Just came to pick up dinner."

Out of the corner of my eyes, I notice the bag on the counter, the name Saint emblazoned on the front of it. Had I not been in such a mood when I walked in, I may have noticed it. As I sit here with him standing silently behind me, I find myself wanting him to turn the chair around, make me face him. I want him to kiss me senseless until I have no other choice but to pick him. To pick us. He does none of it, though. He stands there strong and silent, giving me my space.

"I didn't want this, you know."

"Want what?" I ask.

"You." He chuckles softly. "In fact, I came here to escape everything. Not find more trouble."

"Trouble? Now I'm trouble?" I ask, whipping around on my barstool.

"You've been giving me hell since I stepped foot in this town. For no other reason than because I'm a man, if I remember correctly."

"Not just any man. A man... *the* man who could break me. The one who could leave me irreparable."

Billy shakes his head. "That's not true. No one can break you, Sadie. You're too strong. Too determined. Too much of a fighter to ever let anyone break you. Especially not when it comes to Bryce." Billy takes a slow step toward me. "The thing is, I have no intention of breaking you, let alone hurting you." I begin to speak, but he holds up his hand to stop me. "I know. It's not a guarantee I can make. Just like it isn't one that you can make. We don't know what's going to happen. No one does. What I do know is that we are both determined people. We are both hardworking. And there is no way in hell that either of us would give up on each other without a fight."

"I'm scared."

"Me, too." He pauses for a moment. "When I came to town, I felt empty. I had already lost my mom and grandmother and then the only other thing that mattered to me—my career. I had nothing left. Until I met you. And I'm scared to death of losing you."

I think of every moment with him. How even in hating him, I felt more alive than I have in years. Everything about this man sets something in me on fire. An inexplicable draw feathered by hatred. Hatred that I'm starting to believe really wasn't hatred at all.

"Give me a shot, Sade. Let this be real."

I hate that I hesitate. More than anything, I want to jump into his arms and shout yes. Even with his assurances and kind heart, I can't help the fear that's settled in my belly. It's taken residence and though I am desperately trying to fight it, it's still there.

His fingers brush my cheek. "I'll wait forever if I have to, Sadie. That's how much I believe that what we have is real."

The gentle touch makes my eyes flutter shut. When they open, the entire world seems clearer. His eyes seal my fate. The hopeful smile on his face clearing every last worry from my mind. I rest my hand atop his.

"Yes."

"Really?"

Laughter bubbles over at the surprise I hear in his voice. "For a man that sounded so certain we were destined to be together, you sure as hell look surprised."

"Oh, I'm certain. But you're as damn stubborn as they come. I didn't think it would be that easy."

"Easy? You call these past few months easy?"

He shrugs. "I've been through worse."

Ready to continue our playful banter, I open my mouth to speak, but Billy silences me with a kiss. His lips are warm and gentle, filled with hope and promises. I tangle my hands in his hair, pulling him to me and deepening the kiss. He emits a low growl, his hand on my back pressing me closer to him.

The distinct sound of my grandmother's voice, hooting and hollering, emits from behind the bar.

Our kiss ends, our foreheads resting against each other's.

"About damn time," Grams calls out. "Now, take my granddaughter home and show her just how much you care about her."

"Grams," I say, my face turning beet red.

Not Billy, though. His smile widens; the look in his eye has a sexy but evil glint to it. Before I realize what's happening, he has me over his shoulder and is heading out the door.

I pound gently on his back, begging him to let me go. Fat chance of that.

"Night, Loretta," he calls out as he walks us through the door.

"You've made your point. You can put me down now," I tell him.

Billy sets me on my feet, but his hands never leave me. Our bodies are still pressed against each other. "I'll put you down, but you're crazier than I thought if you think I am ever letting you go."

Chapter 28

Sadie

B liss. Euphoric bliss. That's what these past few weeks with Billy have felt like.

"I don't think I have ever seen you look this happy before," Jules tells me. "You're glowing."

"I am not," I say.

She tugs me in front of a mirror in the store and rests her chin on my shoulder. "That honey, is a glow. And I couldn't be happier for you."

"Why is Mom glowing?" Bryce asks as he rejoins us, holding a few different football books in his hand.

"I'm not. Your aunt Jules is crazy," I tell Bryce, wrapping my arms around him and pulling him against me. "Those the books you want?"

Bryce nods enthusiastically. "They're the exact ones I heard Billy talking about. I can't wait to read them."

There's still a level of fear there, but I love how close the two of them are. Billy seems to gain just as much from Bryce as Bryce does from Billy. It warms my heart to see them interact, to see the love there. And while I can't completely let go of that fear, I know Billy isn't Jon. He's not the kind of man who would just walk away from Bryce regardless of what happens between the two of us. No, Billy is a stand-up guy. One who will make sure he always remains a part of Bryce's life—in one form or another.

"We just need to run to a few more stores," I tell him before taking some money out of my purse and handing it to him to pay for his items.

Bryce scampers off, leaving me to endure Jules on my own. "Quit looking at me like that."

"Quit acting like you aren't falling head over heels in love with Billy."

"I'm not." I pause. "I already have."

Jules squeals loudly, several people in the store turning and looking in our direction.

"Quiet down, will you?" Though, I can't help but find myself laughing at her excitement.

"I knew it. So, when's the wedding?"

I give her a playful shove. "Whoa, back up there. We are nowhere near that stage. And, honestly, I'm not sure that's a path I ever want to go down again."

"What? Seriously? Not even for a man like him?"

"Let's just not go there, okay?"

"Why not? You've let him go everywhere else." She wiggles her eyebrows at me.

"I don't know why I tell you anything," I say, my cheeks flushing with embarrassment.

"Oh, quit acting like such a prude. I'm surprised that Mr. Goody Two-shoes had it in him to tread the uncharted territory."

"What are you guys talking about?" Bryce asks.

"Fishing," I reply.

"Deep sea fishing," Jules pipes in.

"You're bad," I tell her, swatting her arm before heading off to another store.

While Jules and Bryce peruse some racks of clothes, I shoot a quick text to Billy.

Me: Hey.

Billy: Well, hey, gorgeous. How's your shopping trip?

Me: Good. Better if you were here.

Billy: Wish I was.

Me: Maybe you should come to the next one.

Billy: On second thought...

Me: Ah... the truth comes out.

Billy: When will you guys be back?

Me: Miss us already?

Billy: Of course. But I also have a surprise for you.

Me: I'm intrigued.

Billy: Then hurry home.
Billy: XoXo

When we get home a couple hours later, Billy is already there on the porch, waiting for us.

"Well, hey there," I greet him. I step into his embrace and press a chaste kiss to his delicious lips. It's so tempting to do more, but controlling ourselves doesn't seem to be a thing we do anymore. Anything beyond this and Billy's surprise will have to wait for another day.

"Hi, Billy," Bryce shouts from the car where he's helping Jules get the bags out of the trunk.

Billy waves at Bryce, a beaming smile on his face. He turns to me. "Hey, yourself. Got a second?"

"Yeah, of course."

Taking my arm, he leads me to the side of the house.

"Everything okay?" I ask.

"Better than okay." Billy's smiling more than I've ever seen. "Don't get mad, but I kind of did something today. A surprise for Bryce."

"Now I'm worried."

"I got us tickets to a Remington Railcats game and a hotel to stay in for the night. Kind of a back to school gift and first... family outing." There's almost a childlike quality to the way he's smiling. Almost like Bryce on Christmas morning.

"Family outing?" I pause for effect. "I like the sound of that."

Billy looks relieved that I didn't banish the term from use. Especially considering Jon seems to have vanished into thin air again. I'm still not sure what it was he was doing here, but Bryce certainly wasn't the priority.

Not that it mattered much because the man standing before me, he always makes Bryce a priority. Even when I fight him on it.

"You didn't have to go to all this trouble. He'll just be thrilled that we're all together. Like a family."

"I know I didn't have to. But I want to. I like the idea of being able to spoil the two of you. Plus, it would be great to introduce him to some other sports besides football."

"I could kiss you."

"You should. A lot. Later, though. We need to get going or we'll be late."

Billy grabs a few of the bags Bryce is juggling and follows him into the house, muttering "like mother, like son" under his breath.

"I heard that," I call out.

"She hears everything." Bryce groans.

Chapter 29

Billy

J ules left for home, leaving the three of us in the kitchen unpacking the shopping bags.

"Any plans today?" I ask Bryce.

Bryce shrugs. "Tommy went to his aunt's house, so I might hang out with Danny."

"Oh. Cool. That's too bad, though."

"Why?" Bryce asks, giving me a strange look.

"Well, it's just that I had these three tickets to the Remington Railcats game tonight and I—"

Bryce lunges at me and yanks the tickets out of my hand. He stares at them intently. "Wait, what? Is this for real?"

Bryce looks at Sadie for direction. "Billy is taking us to a baseball game in the city. One of his friends plays for the Remington Railcats."

"This is so cool." His face freezes, his eyes widening. "This isn't a date, is it?"

Sadie wraps her arms around Bryce. "I love you, kid. No way are you coming on dates with me and Billy, though."

"Whew."

Biting back my laughter, I tell him, "Go grab your stuff."

***

Bryce steps out of the car, his eyes wide as saucers as he takes in the baseball field. "This place is huge."

"It sure is. Not as big as a football stadium, though."

"Can we go to a football game, too?"

"Bryce," Sadie scolds.

I realize it's in part because she doesn't want her kid asking for things like he did, but I also know it's because she's more than well aware of my fear of football.

What she doesn't seem to get is that when it comes to her and Bryce, I'll make any sacrifice necessary to make them happy.

"Let's just try to enjoy this game first," I tell him. "Come on, there's more to see."

"This is so cool," Bryce says as we step into the box seats I got us. He runs around the room filled with snacks and treats before stopping to stare out at the field where the players are warming up.

"Billy, this is too much," Sadie tells me.

My hands rest on her hips and I tug her close against me. "This isn't any trouble, Sadie. This is my life. I know it can be a lot to get used to, but it's part of who I am."

I can see concern flash over her face.

"Don't do that," I tell her. "Don't read into what I'm saying. I love being in New Hope. I love being with you and Bryce. But this is still a part of me, too."

She nods and smiles, but I can still see the hesitation.

"We can have it all, Sadie. I want to give you the world. And I want that world to be based in New Hope."

"You don't have to say that. This is new and I know that..."

"I love you, Sadie." I blurt the statement out. This isn't how I had intended to say the words to her, but something tells me she needs to hear them. She needs to know so that she can fully understand just how much I care about her, how deeply I want this—us.

"You what? No. You can't."

"I can and I do."

Sadie turns away from me and moves to the buffet bar where she begins to toy with a napkin. I stand behind her, my hands on her hips.

"Why? When? I-I don't know what to say."

I'll admit, her not saying it back doesn't feel great. I also know how cautious she is. How afraid she is—still. "You don't have to say anything, baby. I just wanted you to know I'm all in. I love you and Bryce, and I wouldn't give up what we have for anything."

"Not even the big city, super fancy life you led before coming to New Hope?"

"Not even."

Slowly, she turns to face me. "What if I said that I think I might love you, too?"

She looks up at me, worrying her lip between her teeth. "Then I'd say you made me one happy man."

"Mom, Billy, come look at this," Bryce shouts, interrupting the moment. I don't mind, though. I move out onto the open space with him and scoop him up before setting him on my shoulder.

When the game begins, Bryce settles himself in my lap, questions flying out of him one after another.

"Looks like there's another sport he might like more than football," I whisper to Sadie.

After the Remington Railcats win the game, we head behind the scenes to meet some of the players.

"Holy shit, if it isn't Billy Saint in the flesh." I recognize the voice immediately and begin to laugh.

Turning around, I come face-to-face with Ethan Parks. "Hey, man. Good to see you."

He pulls me in for a quick hug before turning his attention to Sadie. "And who is this beautiful creature?" Ethan reaches for her hand and brings it up to his lips. "Ethan Parks at your service. I assure you I can do anything better than he can."

When his eyes catch a glimpse of an awestruck Bryce, Ethan drops Sadie's hand and turns to me. "Looks like you've been busy."

"Ethan, that's Bryce, Sadie's son," I tell him.

He drops to a knee so he's at Bryce's height. "Nice to meet you, Bryce. I'm Ethan. Did you enjoy the game?"

Bryce nods enthusiastically. I'm pretty sure he's still shell-shocked by the whole experience. I am more than happy to provide it to him.

"I was the best part of it, wasn't I? Did you see that home run I made?" Ethan continues on.

"It went really far," Bryce replies, finally finding his voice.

"Ever played baseball before?" Ethan asks.

Bryce shakes his head. "I play football, for Billy."

Ethan rolls his eyes. "Why don't you let me show you what it's like to play a real sport? What do you say we head down to the field and play some catch? Then maybe you can try some batting practice?"

"That's a very generous offer, but you don't have to do that," Sadie pipes in.

"I know. I'm Ethan Parks and I don't have to do anything I don't want to. And I want to do this, gorgeous. A few other things I'm thinking about doing, too." Ethan throws a smile in Sadie's direction, his eyes roaming her body.

"Back off," I warn him. "She's taken."

"Don't you want what's best for her?" Ethan asks. "We both know I'm the best."

Sadie chokes down her laughter as we make our way down to the field. Bryce has the time of his life running the bases, playing catch with Ethan, and trying to score his own home run.

"As much as I hate to put an end to this," Sadie begins, "it's almost midnight. Bryce really needs to get some sleep."

I nod in agreement and go to break up the fun. When Bryce's face falls, Ethan assures him he can come back anytime.

"Before you go, can we talk for a second?" Ethan asks.

I look at Sadie, who nods her approval. "What's up?"

"What's up? You tell me. You disappear into thin air, you reappear with a gorgeous woman and kid, and you're refusing to give the number one team in the NFL an answer?"

"What are you talking about? What team? What answer?"

"You don't know?"

"Clearly not."

"The New England Jackals want you to come coach for them. Be their defensive coordinator. Do you not have cell service wherever the hell you've been hiding out?"

My mind is completely blown. Everything is starting to make sense now. Jon's presence. The nonstop calls from Tara that I've been ignoring. After her inappropriate advances and what I overheard her say to Sadie at the hospital event, I decided to distance myself from her. By that point, Sadie had become priority and I wasn't going to do anything to jeopardize that.

Most of all, I'm shocked by how much the offer excites me. Part of the reason I had wanted to come to New Hope was to distance myself from football. Not that I had really done a great job of it, what with the youth league and all, but I certainly didn't want any part of the NFL.

"I... So many people were calling, digging, trying to get a story out of me. I blocked all unknown numbers. I was sick of dealing with it."

"Yeah, well, get unsick of it. This is a great opportunity, man."

I'm so stunned by what Ethan's just told me. "Yeah, I, uh... I need time to process. Thanks for giving me a heads-up. And, uh, thanks for tonight. The kid's elated."

"He's a good kid. And his mom could definitely do better."

"Fuck you," I say with a laugh as I pull him in for a hug. "Thanks again."

"Anytime, Coach," he calls after me.

Luckily, Sadie doesn't read anything into the name, assuming, I'm sure, that I told him about the youth league back in New Hope.

Bryce is out cold the minute his head hits the pillow.

When I return to the bedroom, Sadie's lying in the middle of the bed, completely naked, with nothing more than the baseball hat Ethan gave her on.

"You look sexy as hell, but I don't want you wearing other men's clothes."

She bats her eyelashes. "What are you going to do about it?"

I grab her ankles and tug her to the edge of the bed. My hand reaches for the hat and tosses it across the room.

Her legs wrap around me, locking around my waist. "Take your pants off."

"I thought I was the one who gave the orders?" My hand undoes the fly of my pants, and I shove them down to my ankles.

"Not tonight. Got a problem with it?"

"Hell no."

Standing at the edge of the bed, I stroke my cock. She lifts her hips to meet me.

"Fuck me, Billy."

Her body on display for me, hair fanned out around her head, and her pussy glistening. "I have never seen anything more beautiful."

"That's nice. Now, are you going to fuck me or not?"

"You asked for it," I tell her as I slam into her as deep and hard as I can.

Her mouth opens, screams of pleasure about to fall from her lips. My hand covers her mouth as I continue to drive into her. My eyes are glued to her. The way she's touching herself, first her breasts, then sliding down between us.

The sight undoes me. On the brink of pleasure, I quicken the already punishing pace, seeking my release—and hers.

I can feel her pussy tighten around me and know that she's close. "Come for me, Sadie."

As though she was waiting for the order, she begins to shudder, her teeth sinking into the palm of my hand. Watching her orgasm brings my own to fruition. Buried deep inside of her, I give a few last thrusts, emptying into her.

"Jesus Christ, woman. Are you trying to kill me?" I ask as I fall onto the bed next to her.

She rolls on top of me, her lips pressing to mine. "Sweet way to go, though, right?"

I nip at her bottom lip. "The best way. I love you, Sadie."

Chapter 30

Billy

"It all makes sense now," I say into the phone.

"How did I not know about this?" Mason asks. Ever since I told him about the offer from the Jackals, all he's been able to think about is how he was the last to know about it.

"Seriously? Does that really matter right now?"

"No, of course not. I just wish I knew. I could have told you sooner."

"Yeah, well, even with my delay in response, they still seem eager to have me."

"No shit, man. You'd be perfect for the job."

I scrub my hand over my face. "I hate that I'm saying this, but I'm actually kind of excited about it. For so long I wanted nothing to do with football anymore, but I don't know. When Ethan told me about the offer, I just..."

"Football is in your blood, man. Of course an offer like this is going to intrigue you. The question is, are you going to take it?"

"I don't know. I'm meeting with them on Friday to discuss details."

"What about Sadie and Bryce?"

"They're the exact reason I didn't flat out accept."

New England is clear across the country. How would it even work? There is no way Sadie would uproot Bryce from New Hope after all he's been through. I would never even ask that of her. Which means I would have to stay here and turn down the coaching job. A huge part of me wants to take it, though.

"Well, what did she say when you told her?" he inquires.

"I, uh, I haven't told her."

"Dude."

"Give me a break, okay? I'm trying to wrap my head around all this shit. Two days ago, I was perfectly content with the idea of living my life out here with Sadie and Bryce. And now…"

"You have to tell her."

"I know. I will. I just… I want to go to this meeting first. See what they say. If I'm not going to take it, there's no sense in upsetting her."

Mason's laughter rings through the phone. "Take it from me. She'll still be pissed."

Sadie appears in the doorway.

"Hey, Mase, I have to go."

"Tell her," he repeats.

"Bye, Mason." I disconnect the phone and drop it onto the couch. "Hey there."

Sadie walks over to me and wraps her arms around my neck. "Hey, yourself." My lips press against her forehead and linger there a little longer than normal. "Everything okay?"

"Yeah, why wouldn't it be?"

"You seem a little distracted."

"Actually, I am. I, uh… I have to head out to New York for business," I tell her.

"Business in New York? I thought you lived in Wisconsin."

I nod. "I did, but my manager and agency are based out of New York. There are just some loose ends that I need to tie up with them."

"When do you leave?"

I swallow down the guilt that rises in my throat. "Tomorrow."

"Well, then, follow me."

"Follow you? Are you going to give me a special send-off?"

Sadie rolls her eyes at me. "I'm going to give you dinner. With me and Bryce. You in?"

"You bet your fine ass I am," I tell her as I swat her backside.

"Billy," she squeals. "Behave."

I wrap my arms around her from behind. "What can I say, Sadie Hart, you bring out the bad in me."

She tosses her head back in laughter.

***

Sadie is busy working in the kitchen while Bryce and I wrestle on the floor in the living room. Being with Bryce is pure joy. The love I feel for him is incomprehensible. I've loved women before, but this is different. He might not be my kid, but after these past few months, I love him as if he were. Being away from him for the next few days is going to break my heart.

What in the hell would I do if I moved away—permanently?

"As much as I hate to break this up, dinner's almost ready." Sadie's standing in the doorway, a towel slung over her shoulder and a smile on her face that could light the whole damn town.

"Aw. Mom," Bryce whines.

"Go wash up," I tell him. "We'll rematch after dinner."

Bryce does as instructed, running off to wash his hands, giving me the opportunity to put my hands on his mother. I make my way over to her. "You look happy."

"I am happy. Happier than I've ever been, actually."

"Me too." My hands reach up to cup her face and bring her lips to mine in a tender kiss.

"What was that for?" she asks.

"Because I'm going to miss the hell out of you the next couple days."

"We're going to miss you, too."

"You're leaving?" Bryce asks. I can hear the terror in his voice, and it breaks my heart.

Fuck.

"No, buddy, not like that. I just have to go out of town for a couple days. I'll be back Sunday," I explain, trying to lessen some of the pain I see in his eyes.

"That's what Dad said and—"

"Bryce, honey, it's not the same. Billy isn't leaving for a job. He's going to tie up some loose ends so he can stay here. Right, Billy?"

"She's right," I tell him. I hate that I'm lying to him—to them. His reaction only solidifies my decision. Until I know what it is that I'm doing, there is no way in hell I'm telling anyone. "I'll be back before you know it."

Bryce still looks hesitant. I wish I knew what to do to make this easier on him. I look at Sadie for direction, but she looks just as clueless as I am.

Pulling out my phone from my pocket, I pull up my ticket. "See here," I say, pointing to the screen. "What does that say?"

"Round trip."

"Right. Do you know what that means?"

"Your trip is round?" Bryce guesses.

"Kind of." I chuckle. "What it means is that I have a ticket to fly to New York. And one to fly back—a round trip. It goes both ways. See, I have to come back. While I'm gone, I need a favor. Think you can help me with it?"

Bryce nods. "Sure."

I lean in close to Bryce so Sadie can't hear. "I need you to get some flowers for your mom and give them to her from me. Think you can do that?"

He nods.

"Thanks, bud."

When dinner is over and Bryce is wrestled out, me and Sadie take him upstairs and tuck him in. "I'll see you in a few days. And don't forget what I asked." I nod toward the dresser where I dropped a twenty for him.

"I'm on it," he promises me.

I press a kiss to the top of his head. "Love you, kiddo."

His smile is so big it looks as though it could reach the ends of the earth. "I love you too, Billy."

I shut the door to his room, and I hate myself more now than I did when they said I would never play again.

Sadie's arms wrap around my waist. "What's wrong?"

I press my lips to her forehead. "Nothing. Just going to miss you guys. That's all."

"Come on," she says, taking my hand and leading me to her bedroom. "Let's say goodbye properly."

Chapter 31

Sadie

The sight of Jon standing on my doorstep causes me to groan. "What are you doing back?"

Jon had disappeared without a word. Not even so much as a goodbye to Bryce.

"Can I come in?"

I shake my head. "Bryce isn't here."

I move to shut the door, but his hand stops it. "I'm not here to see Bryce."

"Then what are you doing here? We have nothing else to say to each other. Nothing to discuss if it isn't about Bryce."

"I beg to differ. We have plenty to talk about. Like your boyfriend."

"I don't care what you have to say, Jon. Not about Billy, not about anything, really. Why don't you just slink away into the night and never come back?"

Jon ignores me and my attempt to keep him out of the house. He pushes past me and takes a seat on the couch. If he weren't Bryce's father, I would throw his ass out in a heartbeat. But on the off chance that Bryce returns unexpectedly, I don't want to cause any issues.

"Billy and I know each other."

"Yeah, I know." While initially it hadn't dawned on me, I realized how much contact the two of them must have had with Jon following the league around for his stories.

"What you might not know is how well we know each other."

"Is that what this is about? Did I steal your crush from you?"

Jon rolls his eyes. "Joke all you want, but you're going to want to hear this."

I groan. "Just say what you came to say and leave."

"When I left, the television station I worked for had me traveling all over, following different teams."

"Yay for you."

Ignoring my sarcasm, he continues. "I spent a lot of time with the players. I became one of the guys."

He pauses, waiting for some type of response from me.

"I spent a lot of time with the players. Billy included."

"Will you just spit it out already?"

"Billy dated Mara. That means you're not the only woman we've shared."

I roll my eyes. "We all have pasts. I already know he dated her, if you can even call it that, and I don't care. He certainly doesn't hold my marriage to you against me."

Jon continues on. "Well, did you know he introduced me to Mara? In fact, he offered her up to me. Handed over the keys—if you know what I mean."

I drop the towel I had been folding.

"That's right," Jon continues. "Not only did he date her, he introduced me to her."

"No." My head is spinning, trying to wrap my mind around what Jon's saying while at the same time disputing any truth behind it. Jon's just trying to get a rise out of me. Billy would have told me if that were true.

"It's true," Jon says. He drops a photo of the three of them on the table, Mara between them.

"That doesn't prove anything."

"Do you know where your boyfriend is this weekend?" Jon asks.

"Yes, and it's none of your business."

"I don't need you to tell me, Sade. I know where he is. And I know why he's there."

Jon extends his phone in my direction. Curiosity gets the best of me and I take it from him. It's an email from Reese Holland, Jon's boss.

"Saint is in New England to sign the contract for the coaching job. If you want your job back, get your ass there and scoop the story."

I stare at the phone, unable to peel my eyes away from the words on the screen. "This can't be right."

"It's right, Sadie."

I throw the phone at him. "Why are you telling me this? Why are you trying to destroy my happiness? Why, Jon?"

"This has nothing to do with you, Sadie. That guy that you think is so wonderful? The one who has been lying to you and our son for months? He's nothing but an asshole. A fraud. A dick." Jon gets up from the couch and paces the room. "We had an agreement. And he backed out of it. Packed his shit and disappeared. It was going to be the story of a lifetime. And thanks to him, I lost my job."

"Oh my God," I exclaim. "So, all of this, it's about your job? You're willing to hurt your own son because of a stupid job?"

"Because I want to make Saint suffer. You and Bryce—"

"Are just collateral damage?" I shake my head in disbelief. "You're a real piece of work."

I storm to the door and yank it open. "Get out."

"Sadie—"

"I said, get out," I yell. Jon laughs as he steps through the door. "Go get your stupid story and stay the fuck away from my son."

I slam the door shut and lock it behind me. I slide to the ground, tears flowing freely.

How could Jon do this to me?

How could Billy?

Chapter 32

Billy

"Thanks for meeting with us, Mr. Saint," Thomas, the owner of the Jackals, says as he offers me a hand.

I shake it before taking my seat across from him. "Thank you for the opportunity, sir."

"Let's get to it, shall we?" Thomas suggests. He's flanked on one side by the head coach and on the other by the offensive coordinator.

The meeting lasts well over two hours, not including the tour of the stadium.

Thomas slides a paper across the table. "Here's our offer."

I glance down at it, the number more than generous. "Wow."

"That's the reaction we were hoping for," Thomas says with a hearty laugh.

"When I got your offer," I begin, "I hadn't even thought about coaching. In fact, I wanted to avoid football altogether."

"That's understandable," Thomas says.

"The thing is, I'm already a coach. It doesn't pay well." I chuckle. "In fact, it doesn't pay at all. As much as I appreciate your offer, I don't think I can leave my current team."

In return, I slide him the picture of the New Hope Saints. He looks down at the photo, then back up at me.

"No offer I make could compare to this," he says.

"No, it couldn't."

Thomas stands from the table and extends his hand to me. "If anything changes..."

"I'll keep you mind, of course."

We shake hands and part ways.

Phone in hand, I switch my flight from Sunday to today. I need to get back home.

The minute I stepped on the plane to head to New England, my mind was already made up. Leaving Sadie and Bryce was the hardest thing I ever had to do. Way harder than not playing football again. Even if we could figure out a way for it to work, it wouldn't be enough. Nothing would be. Nothing except being with them. They are enough. They are my world.

With my flight switched, there's one stop I need to make before heading home.

"The nearest jewelry store," I tell the driver.

"Um... Tiffany's?" he says.

"Perfect."

***

"Honey, I'm home," I call out as I step into Sadie's house.

Home.

Over this past week, one thing became certain to me: Home is wherever Sadie and Bryce are. And it's the only place I want to be.

When my eyes land on Sadie, I panic. She's sitting on the couch, her knees tugged at her chest. Jules at her side.

"What is it? What's wrong?" I ask, the things running through my head only getting progressively worse.

"Why don't you tell us?" a very angry Jules snaps back.

I don't know where her anger is coming from or why it's directed at me. I move toward Sadie, taking a seat next to her on the couch. "Will someone tell me what's going on? Baby, what is it? What's wrong?"

I go to wrap my arm around Sadie, but she pushes me away and moves off the couch. Her body trembles as she makes her way to the window. "I thought you were different."

"I don't follow."

"Of course not. Got hit in the head with a football one too many times, hotshot?" Jules barks out at me.

"What the fuck is your problem, Jules?" There's no anger in my voice, only complete and utter confusion.

"You," Jules says, getting to her feet and standing between me and Sadie.

"Jules, stop. I need to talk to Billy. Alone," Sadie tells her.

"Are you sure?" Jules glares at me, refusing to move until Sadie replies. "Fine. You call me if you need me."

With one last look in my direction, Jules steps out of the house.

"I thought you were a good guy. A guy who wouldn't lie or cheat or scheme."

"I am. I'm not."

I make my way to her, my hands reaching for her. The moment my fingers graze her arms, she pulls away again. "Don't touch me."

I retract my hand. I can smell her shampoo. I can feel the heat of her body. Fuck, I can feel the ache in her chest and yet I have no clue what it is that she thinks I did to put it there. "Baby, talk to me."

"Me? Don't you think there are a few things you should be telling me?" Her voice rises, the words reverberating through the room. "Like just how well you know my ex-husband? How you guys were friends? How you set him up with Mara?"

Fuck.

"Or would you prefer to start by telling me what you were doing in New York? Or was it New England, Coach?"

"Sadie, let me explain."

"You had months to explain, Billy. Like when we first ran into Jon at the bar? Or when he showed up at my house? Or how about before you left? You had all this time to talk—why not then?" She laughs a little. "Oh, that's right, because you hadn't been caught. And for whatever reason, you didn't think you would be. You didn't think your pal Jon would rat you out, did you?"

"It's not like that."

"I don't give a damn what it's like. What you did is inexcusable."

"I should have told you. About all of it. I'm sorry. I just—"

"Just what, Billy? Didn't want me to find out that you're the reason my marriage ended? You're the reason that Bryce's father left him? That you were planning on leaving us too?"

"I would never leave you, Sadie."

"But you would ruin my marriage?"

"I didn't do that either. I'm not responsible for Jon's actions. Yes, I introduced him to Mara, but—"

Sadie throws her hands in the air. "There are no buts. You did it. You ruined everything for me."

"I didn't ruin shit," I say, frustration taking over. "I had no idea he was married or had a kid. The guy never wore a ring. He walked around flirting with every woman he could find."

Sadie's body tenses at the words. The reality of what Jon did, the truth behind just how much he was truly unfaithful to her, setting in. While I hate to see the hurt in her eyes from it, I also can't just stand by and let her blame me for something I didn't do.

Keeping the truth from her was wrong and I am more than well deserving of that anger. But there's more to it than that. She's trying to blame me for her marriage falling apart. And that I didn't do.

"I shouldn't have kept it from you. And I should have been upfront about why I went to New England. I just didn't see the point in—"

"Being honest with me?"

"This, Sadie. You blaming me. You being upset. All for nothing. I didn't take the job in New England and I sure as hell didn't force Jon to cheat on his wife."

"It doesn't matter." She marches to the front door and pulls it open. "Get out."

"Like hell it doesn't. I'm not leaving until we finish talking."

"Oh, believe me, we're finished." She stands there, holding the door open. "I said, get out."

"I'm sorry I kept the truth from you, Sadie. I should have been upfront with you. But face it. I'm not the one you're really mad at here." I pause. "Don't take out Jon's infidelity on me. I may have introduced him to Mara, but he's the one who cheated. The one who left. I'm the one who's choosing to stay. The one who's choosing you."

She remains silent, tears welling in her eyes, but the stubborn woman is damn adamant about not letting them fall.

I step out of the house because she needs me to, not because I want to.

"I'm not going anywhere, Sadie. Not now. Not ever. I will be right next door. Waiting for you. For as long as it takes."

Chapter 33

Sadie

It's been two weeks since I ended things with Billy.

Holding true to his words, he's still here. The article on the front page of the sports section that someone left on my doorstep informed me that he had, in fact, turned down the coaching job. He's still here in New Hope. No indication that he'll be leaving anytime soon. In fact, it's quite the opposite. The summer football program is coming to an end and from what I've heard, the fall program is looking even more promising. And Billy is at the helm of all of it.

The article wasn't the only thing that's been left on my porch.

While Billy has maintained his distance from me and Bryce, he sure as hell has made his presence known. Whether it be flowers or chocolate croissants, there's something new on the porch every day.

Today's package is a little different. Today, it requires my signature.

"What is it?" Jules asks.

"I have no clue," I say as I close the door.

She grabs the envelope from my hand and inspects it. "Are you sure it's from Billy? This looks way more official. Legal even. Oh God, what if Jon is filing for custody?"

"It's from Billy," I say, sliding my finger under the opening. "You really think Jon's going to file for custody?"

The notion is beyond comical. The man has no interest in his son. Only work and revenge.

I pull the documents out of the envelope. Jules is right. They are definitely official. "Oh my God," I gasp, my hand flying to my mouth.

The name Jack Roth is the first thing that pops out at me when I look at the document. The next thing I see is the word foundation. Interest piqued, I start at the top of the document and read through it.

"What? What is it? Was I right?" Jules peers over my shoulder and reads the same words I am. "Well, hot damn. Go, Billy."

"Changing teams, Jules?"

"He put together a foundation for sick kids and names it after your favorite patient. Hell yeah, I'm team Billy. Again."

"Traitor."

With the papers in hand, I storm over to Billy's house and pound on the door. Before he can even speak, I start waving the papers in his face. "What the hell is this? Some way to try and buy my forgiveness?"

"You think I did all this in less than two weeks?" Billy chuckles. "I wish I were that good, but I'm not. No, I started this after Jack..." Billy's voice trails off. "I just wanted to do something to make his life even more meaningful than it was. I thought you would be happy."

"I am happy," I say as tears flow down my face. "But I'm also miserable. I..."

"Me, too."

"Why did you do it, Billy? Why weren't you just upfront with me? Why did you have to lie? Why did you have to be like him?"

Tears stream down my face.

"I was scared. I was so scared of losing you. I-I had already lost everything else in my life that I ever loved. My mom. My grandmother. Football. I couldn't bear to lose you, too. It was stupid. I know that."

"You still lost me."

"Isn't there anything I can do to win you back? Anything, Sadie. You name it. I'll do it. You're it for me. You and Bryce."

"After Jon, I had a hard enough time trusting people. I wouldn't let anyone in—you know that. But I trusted you. With my heart. And my son. And you... you trampled all over it. I'm sorry, Billy. I love you, but—"

"We're over?"

I nod.

His hand comes behind my head in a gentle touch as he presses his lips to his forehead. "You changed my life, Sadie. I'll never forget that. And I'll never leave you. I'll always be here if you need me."

His words shatter the already broken pieces of my heart. The only man who could break my heart, just did. The pieces shattered beyond repair with no hope of being able to be put back together.

"Goodbye, Billy."

The minute I get home, I run into Jules's arms. "It's over. It's really over."

"Oh, honey."

Jules holds me tightly as I cry into her hair.

Chapter 34

Billy

If I thought having to give up my football career was hard, it is nothing compared to having to walk away from the only woman I've ever loved.

"You sure about this?" Jules asks.

She's still angry with me for hurting Sadie, but ever the professional, there is no way in hell she was going to pass up the commission I offered her.

"Positive." I sign my name on the dotted line for the millionth time.

The condo I had scoped out as a city getaway for me, Sadie, and Bryce is now officially becoming my home.

I'm keeping my home in New Hope because I'm not ready to give up just yet. Never say never.

Right now, Sadie needs space. So that's what I'm giving her. If I'm honest, living next door to her and not being able to touch her was torture. Even worse were the longing looks Bryce gave me.

"She's miserable, you know?" Jules tells me as she follows me out of the room.

"Butt out, Jules."

She grabs my arm and jerks me around. "You know I can't do that. Jesus, you two are so damn stubborn. You love her. She loves you. Figure it out."

I cock an eyebrow at her. "You're going to give me relationship advice when you've been ignoring your own for years?"

She begins to argue but knows damn well I'm right. "This isn't about me. It's about Sadie and how much she loves you."

"I love her too, Jules. You know that. She's not ready to forgive me yet. I don't know if she ever will be. Watching her and Bryce day in and day out and not being able to be with them? It's killing me. And her."

"Instead, you're going to do exactly what you swore you wouldn't? You're going to leave? What do you think that's going to prove to her?"

"I'm not leaving her," I argue. She's not mine to leave anymore. "I'm cutting my losses and giving us some space because not walking away would just hurt us more. And the last thing I want is to hurt Sadie."

"Well, let me tell you, she's hurting."

I clench my fists at my sides. "I'm doing what's best."

"For whom?" Jules asks.

"For all of us. Me. Sadie. Bryce."

There's a pang in my chest as I say his name. Loving and missing Sadie is one thing. Bryce is a whole other level. He might not be my kid, but he sure as hell stole my heart. I miss him, his smile, the way he rambles on about nonsensical things.

"Well, doing what's best is making all of you miserable. Congrats on that." Jules takes my hand and opens it, dropping the set of keys to the condo into it. "Have fun running away and hiding. Again."

Standing in the middle of the living room, I look around at the empty space. What the fuck have I done? How did things go so sideways?

My phone rings and while I still hope against hope every time that it's Sadie, deep down I know it isn't.

"Hey, Tara," I say. The woman might be an incessant flirt and have some boundary issues, but she's damn good at her job. With Sadie and Bryce out of my life, I needed to find new purpose. I reached out to Tara, asked her to look into a few things for me, and the sound of her voice has me anxious to hear what she's come up with.

"Hey there, handsome. Everything all wrapped up with the condo?"

"Sure is. Any news for me?"

"Only the best news."

"Don't keep me in suspense."

"Okay, it's not a high-ranking spot, but"—she pauses for effect —"the Red Devils would love for you to join their team as a defensive line coach. It's definitely not as much money, or as good of a deal as—"

"I'll take it."

"Are you sure about this, Billy? There are so many opportunities out there for you."

"None are an hour's drive away from New Hope."

"What is with you and the silly little town?" she asks.

"It's home."

I can practically hear her eyes roll through the phone. "Fine. I'll set up the deal with the Devils. Oh, your furniture will be there tomorrow. Make sure you're available for placement. And the gala is this weekend. Still planning on attending alone? Or are you finally going to take me up on my offer as your plus one?"

"Alone. Anything else?"

Tara sighs. "Nope. You're all set."

"Thanks, Tara." I disconnect the line.

Pumping my fist into the air, I celebrate. Tara's right, this job with the Red Devils certainly isn't as fancy a spot as what the Jackals offered me. It's so much better. I'm close to New Hope. I get to work with Mason and Hunter. It's more than I could have hoped for.

Every fiber of my being wants to reach out and call Sadie. A text isn't completely out of the question, though, right?

Me: Hey, Sadie. Just wanted you to hear it from me first. I took a job with the Red Devils as a defensive line coach.

I hit send and await her reply. Not that long ago, they used to be instantaneous. Now, it feels like an eternity.

Sadie: Good for you.

At least she responded, though.

Me: I miss you.

I wait, but nothing comes.

Me: Will you be attending the gala for Jack's foundation on Saturday?

Come on, Sadie, give me something here. Anything.

Sadie: Not sure.

Me: I hope to see you there.

Sadie: Please, stop.

Me: Ok. Sorry.

Chapter 35

Sadie

"I get what he was trying to do. It's just too little too late," I tell Jules.

We're in the hotel room we got in Remington, getting ready for the gala tonight. I hadn't wanted to come, but when Jack's parents asked if I would be attending, how could I say no?

After all, I am the co-chair of the foundation.

"Okay, I get it. The guy fucked up. Big time. But you said yourself that he fucks really good. And doesn't a good fuck outweigh a little fuck-up?"

"Do you even hear yourself when you say these things?" It's the first time in a long time that I've been able to laugh when the discussion even remotely involved Billy.

"Tell me it doesn't make perfect sense?"

I shake my head. "Even if I could forgive him, how am I supposed to trust him again?"

Staring into the mirror, I touch up mascara as I wait for her to give me some sort of ridiculous advice.

"I broke up with Travis," Jules says.

"What are you talking about?"

"I told you he was a jerk who broke my heart. It's the other way around. I'm the jerk. I broke his heart."

"Why didn't you tell me?"

"Because it's my secret. One I didn't want anyone to know. Not even you."

"Jules..." I reach to hug her, but she pulls back.

"I kept the truth from you, Sadie. We shouldn't be friends anymore."

I stop in my tracks, my face falling. "I know what you're doing and it's not the same. Your secret didn't involve me."

"I thought you said the issue was trusting him? You're upset because he kept things from you and now you can't trust him."

"I did the same thing, Sadie. Do you not trust me anymore?"

"Of course I do. It's different. It's—"

"The only difference is Billy has a dick and I suck them. Other than that, it's the same thing."

"Do you want me to be angry?"

"No, of course not. I want you to realize that people make mistakes. But that you are capable of forgiving them. Me, for example. Why not Billy? Why hasn't everything he's done these past several weeks earned your forgiveness?"

"I-I don't know."

"Is it him you can't forgive? Or is it someone else?"

I close my eyes as I let her words settle over me. When I open them, they land on the clock. "Shit, we're going to be late."

I step into the ballroom on unsure feet. Jules is at my side to balance me.

As excited as I am for this event, I'm equally terrified. I know Billy will be here and I'm not quite sure I'm ready to face him yet. Especially not after the conversation Jules and I just had.

"Sadie," I hear a voice call out.

I turn to see Avery waving at me. I plaster a smile on my face. As nice as it is to see her again, where Avery is, so is Mason. And that means Billy's probably nearby, too. Gathering my courage, I head toward her.

"Avery, it's so good to see you." She pulls me in for a hug. "This is my best friend, Jules."

"Nice to meet you, Jules," Avery says as they shake hands.

"You too," Jules agrees.

Avery looks around the ballroom. "Pretty impressive, huh?"

My gaze follows the same path she did as I take in the ambiance of the ballroom. It's beautifully decorated. Every detail in place. Not only that, but there are stars and politicians—a literal who's who.

"It's amazing. I can't believe he did all this."

"He was extremely hands on with it. Involved in every detail," Avery tells me.

"I'm sure. He needed a new purpose. At least this time he picked a worthwhile cause."

"Oh, I don't know. I think the house was a pretty worthwhile cause. It led him to you after all."

I laugh. "Yeah, that worked out well."

Avery loops her arm through mine as she walks me through the room. "No one said your story has to be over yet. God knows mine and Mason's has had more twists and turns than most."

"It's over," I assure her. The notion truly settles over me when I see Billy standing and talking to a gorgeous—young—woman.

"Only if you let it be." Avery stops a few feet from where Billy is standing with the woman. "Billy made a mistake. A stupid mistake. We all do. But he's a good guy—the best. And if you love him half as much as I think you do, you're going to want to fight for him."

She gives me a slight shove in his direction.

"Sadie? Is that you?" The surprise in his voice is evident and confusing.

"Did you really think I would miss all this?" I ask with a smile.

The woman next to him is glaring at me. Looks like I stepped up at just the right time.

"Jules said—"

"I changed my mind."

Whatever was going on between him and the unknown woman is long forgotten. His focus is solely on me.

"I'm glad you did. You look... spectacular."

"Thanks." The comment causes heat to rise to my cheeks and anger to flash through the eyes of the woman next to him.

"I didn't mean to interrupt," I say, finally acknowledging the woman.

"You didn't," he tells me.

The woman clears her throat, finally catching Billy's attention. "Sorry, Val. I need to speak with Sadie, alone."

He rests his hand on the small of my back and ushers me toward a doorway.

"I really didn't mean to interrupt. I just—"

"You really didn't. If anything, you saved me."

"Getting bombarded by women?" I ask with a hint of amusement.

"Something like that."

A moment later, we're alone in a small office just outside of the ballroom. The room fills with a heaviness from tension and desire.

"How have you been?" We both ask the question simultaneously.

"You first," he tells me.

"Truthfully?"

Billy nods.

"Miserable. I've been angry and sad and frustrated and just plain miserable. You?"

"Same."

We stare at each other for a moment. Both of us unsure of where we go from here.

"Fuck it," Billy blurts out.

"Huh?"

His hand reaches for me, pulling me flush against him. Warm, soft lips crash against mine. The kiss is a tender push and pull that speaks volumes more than words could say. My fingers grip the lapels on his tuxedo, holding him close. When his tongue runs along the seam of my lips, begging for entrance, I don't even hesitate to let him in.

The kiss ends, Billy resting his forehead against mine.

"This doesn't change anything," I inform him.

"Maybe not, but it sure as hell feels good. I've missed you, Sadie."

I hesitate but realize that the biggest issue with us has been honesty. So, I tell him the truth. "I've missed you, too. So much."

"I'm glad the feeling's mutual." Billy pauses for a moment. "What do you say we make the rounds and get out of here? There's something I want to show you."

"I don't know."

"Please, Sadie. Give me tonight and then, if you want, I'll leave you alone. For good."

Even though I hate the permanence in his words—for good—I know they're for the best.

Tenderly, I reach up and touch his face. "One last night."

He covers my hand with his and leans into it. We stay like this for a moment before he moves my hand and presses a kiss to my palm. "Shall we?"

Looping my arm through his, we step back into the ballroom.

Chapter 36

Billy

"Are you going to give me a clue about this thing you want to show me?" Sadie asks.

We're standing outside the banquet center, waiting for the limo to pick us up. "One clue. That's it. It's a place."

"That's not a clue," she argues.

"Yes, it is."

"It's not a good clue."

"You didn't ask for a good clue," I tease.

A moment later, the limo pulls up and I slide in next to her.

"Ever had sex in a limo?" I ask her.

"No. And I won't be doing it tonight, either." Sadie smirks as she crosses her legs and clasps her hands in front of me.

"If you're trying to torture me, you're doing a damn good job of it," I tell her as my eyes scrape over her legs, her chest, and land on her eyes.

"Billy..." My name is nothing more than an exhale.

"I think you're lying to yourself if you think we're not making love tonight, Sadie." My hand drops to her thigh, sliding up the soft skin until my fingers toy with the hem of her dress, but goes no further.

Her gaze drops to my hand. Watching. Waiting.

"You're calling the shots tonight, Sadie. Decide."

Her hand covers mine in a will she, won't she move. Either she pushes it away or slides it up. The choice is hers.

"Sex won't fix what's broken."

I'm not sure if the statement is for her benefit or mine.

She moves my hand up and under her skirt. "Take the long way," I tell the driver before closing the partition.

"At least one part of you misses me," I tease as I run my finger over the wet fabric of her panties. She rests her head back, her thighs parted.

My fingers slide under the satin fabric until the only silk I feel is that of her soft, wet folds. Her hand reaches for me, undoing the button, then sliding the zipper down until she can slide her hand inside.

"Stop." The minute the words fall from her lips, I pull my hand back, an apology falling from my lips.

"I need more," Sadie tells me. "I need you."

Her legs flank my hips, her dripping wet pussy pressed against my cock.

Her mouth is on mine, hard and hot. My cock sinks into her pussy.

Desperate.

It's the only word to describe how this moment feels.

She rocks her hips back and forth, my cock feeling like it's hitting the ends of the Earth inside her. My hands tangle in her hair, pulling it back and exposing her neck.

Hard and fast, we move together, both filled with want, both needing more than just the release this moment is going to bring.

She needs closure. I need her.

"Fuck, Sadie," I cry out as my orgasm hits.

"Billy," she screams as she rides out her own wave of pleasure.

When our high subsides and the limo slows, her head is buried in my shoulder, sobbing.

I hold her tightly, not wanting to say goodbye. Not wanting to let go.

"Baby..."

She lifts her head and presses a finger to my lips. "Show me."

We manage to put ourselves back together before the driver opens the door. I tip him more than generously and thank him for his time.

"What is this place?" Sadie asks. I love the satisfied, sexed-up look she's rocking at the moment.

"You'll see. Come on." Lacing my fingers through hers, I lead her through the lobby and then to the elevator. I press the button for the top floor.

She steps off the elevator and into the condo gingerly. "You bought a condo."

"I did."

"Congratulations. It's beautiful."

"I would have told you sooner, but—"

"It's none of my business."

"I wanted it to be a surprise."

"I'm definitely surprised," she tells me as she makes her way over to the floor-to-ceiling windows.

"Then let me really blow your mind. I bought it for us."

"Us?"

"I put in the offer before we left after the baseball game. I wanted to surprise you and Bryce. Give us a home to stay at whenever we came to the city rather than a hotel."

I'm not sure what I expected her to say or even how I thought she would react, but I didn't anticipate no response at all. An uncomfortable silence settles over us and I'm not sure exactly how to break it.

"I'm sorry, Billy," Sadie blurts out. Her back is to me, her gaze focused on the city before her.

I wait for the rest. The part where she tells me she's sorry she came to Remington. And even more that she's sorry she came back here with me.

"I never should have pushed you away." Her words stun me. I don't expect them, or the apology. I'm the one who fucked things up.

"You don't have anything to be sorry for. I'm the one who owes you the apology."

Sadie faces me, her head shaking. "You already apologized. And it wasn't until tonight when I saw you that I realized I had already forgiven you. You were right, Billy. It's not you that I was upset with. It was Jon. I took out the anger I had for him on you because, unlike him, you stuck around. You were there for me to be angry with. It wasn't fair to you."

I still don't want or need the apology, but I know Sadie well enough to know she needs to do her thing. "It's okay, baby."

"No, it isn't. From the moment you walked into my life, I projected every ounce of hurt, every ounce of pain and anger that

Jon made me experience onto you. You were my punching bag, all while saving me at the same time."

"I'd do it again in a heartbeat."

"Why? What did I do to deserve you? The way you treat me? There are a million women out there..."

"And none of them hold a candle to you, Sadie. And they sure as hell don't make me feel the way you do."

"Are Bryce and I going to be enough? Because this, Billy, this is what I picture when I see you." She spins around slowly, her arms extended for emphasis.

"Really? Because I was thinking about how much I loved being in New Hope. That sitting on the swing with you, your hand in mine? That was one of my favorite things to do."

"What about your new coaching job?"

"It's right here in Remington. For the Red Devils. It doesn't pay much, but it's close. I can commute back and forth. No problem."

The look on her face says she wants to believe me. The look in her eyes says she's afraid to.

"When I left Wisconsin to come to New Hope, I did it because I needed a purpose. Something to fill the gaping hole that not being able to play football left in me. I thought fixing that house would help me heal. One look at you and I knew I was wrong. That house wasn't going to save me. You were. We were going to save each other."

I pull the blue box out of my pocket where it's been since I bought it.

"Look at me, Sadie," I tell her. She turns, her head tilting up to look at me.

Her gaze drops to the ground. "What are you doing?"

"What I've wanted to do since I turned down that stupid job in New England. I'm proposing to you, Sadie." I flick the box open, showing the sparkling diamond I handpicked for her. "You're my purpose in life. You and Bryce. You're my world and I can't imagine a life without you in it."

"Billy..."

"I know it's kind of quick, especially since we've been apart for weeks. We can get married tonight or wait a million years. I don't care. I just want to know that we're not over. I want to know we have a chance."

Her hand gently touches my face. "Never say never. Yes, Billy. I will marry you. Tonight, tomorrow. Name the time. Name the place. I'm there."

I stand up and pull her into my arms, pressing a kiss to her lips.

"I completely forgot to give you the tour."

"Seriously? You're worried about giving me a tour? Now?"

I toss her over my shoulder. "Yep. First and only stop... the bedroom."

Epilogue

Sadie | One year later...

I jump from my seat, screaming my head off as Bryce scores his second touchdown of the game. He does a little dance in the end zone, and I can't help but giggle. Despite the confidence he's exuding, he still looks so silly.

It's the Super Bowl and my kid is the quarterback.

Who would have thought?

A year ago, I refused to even let him play. Now he's tearing up that field and loving every minute of it. And I have Billy to thank for all of it.

I watch them huddled together on the field, going over something in the playbook. My heart swells at the sight. Just like it does every time I see them together. Billy has proven to be a better father than Bryce's own biological father ever was. He's attentive and involved. So affectionate. After a year without a single call or visit, I'm fairly certain that Jon is out of our lives for good. From the looks of it, it doesn't seem like Bryce really minds anymore.

It's hard to believe it's only been a year. A year since Billy walked into our lives, since I fell for him—since we fell apart. I'm so grateful that we found our way back to each other. And even more grateful that Billy insisted on moving in with me and Bryce the moment we returned to New Hope. He said we had wasted enough time during our breakup and that he was never letting me out of his sight again.

The rest... is history. Pure, blissful, history.

The players retake the field just as Jules and Grams take the seat next to me.

"About time you two showed up," I say. "You missed Bryce's touchdown."

"No doubt he'll have another from what Travis said." The statement falls from Jules's lips like it's the most natural thing in the world.

I whip my head in her direction—pleasantly confused. "Oh, is that what Travis says?"

"Don't make a big deal out of it. We're talking. That's it." Jules blows off the question, trying to be nonchalant about her little slip-up.

"From what I've heard, most of their 'talking' has been done horizontally," Grams chimes in. For once, I'm glad it's Jules on the chopping block and not me.

With our eyes focused on the game, Grams and I continue to pry about Travis. The more we poke around, the more flustered she becomes until she finally blurts out that she loves him. At the exact moment, the field goes quiet. Everyone's head whips in her direction, including Travis's.

"About time, Jules," he calls out to her from the field. "I love you, too. Now, shut up. We're in the middle of a game here."

Her cheeks are fiery red, but the smile on her face is undeniable. Jules stands up, blows Travis a kiss, and then tells everyone in the stands to mind their own business and watch the game.

"Well, this game certainly got more interesting," I say, trying to hide my laughter.

"You have no idea," Jules mumbles.

"What's that?" I ask.

Grams' elbow connects with Jules's side. She lets out a small yelp. "Pay attention to the game."

The game is nearing its end. The Saints are in the lead, but the Devils aren't far behind. We're down to the wire. With the ball in his hands, Bryce lifts his arm. And as all the kids scramble, he yanks his arm back down, tucks it to his side, and runs at top speed.

Thirty.

Twenty.

Ten.

Touchdown.

The clock runs out. The game is over.

Saints win the Super Bowl.

As I stand in my spot, watching Billy with Bryce on his shoulders, tears well in my eyes. It's the most beautiful picture, the most perfect day.

I notice Bryce has something in his hands, above his head. It's a sign. They move a little closer and after wiping the tears from my eyes, I'm finally able to make out what it says.

How about today?

How about today, what? I'm stuck in the middle of a roaring crowd, unable to make my way to them to find out what the hell it is he's talking about.

Travis stands next to Billy and hands him a microphone.

"What do you say, Sadie?" Billy asks.

"About what?" I shout back.

"When I proposed, you told me to name the time and the place and that you'd be there. They told me I would never play football again and yet, somehow, I managed to score the perfect touchdown. So, what do you say? Marry me today?"

Jules whispers in my ear, "I've got you a dress and flowers. Say yes, Sadie."

As if I could ever say no to him?

"Yes," I shout before pushing through the crowd and running into his arms.

He kisses me slow and sweet as Bryce groans from his spot on Billy's shoulders.

"You're unbelievable."

"This is a pretty momentous occasion."

"Really? I mean, I've already done this once," I tease.

"Yeah, but you didn't do it right."

"Bryce wanted to walk you down the aisle," Billy tells me.

"What aisle?" I ask, laughing.

Only, I had been so lost in him, in our moment, that I hadn't noticed what was actually happening on the field. The aisle runner. The chairs. The flowered arch that seemed to appear out of nowhere. Our friends scattered around—Mason and Avery, Hunter and Quinn, Grams and Jules.

"Billy..."

"But I told him that his mom is really good at standing on her own two feet. I, however, wouldn't be able to do this without my best guy by my side. Hope you don't mind that I stole him and made him my best man."

"No one better to give the honor to." I look up at Bryce. "You good with this, kiddo? Me marrying Billy, being a family? All of it?"

"I thought we already were?"

"We are," I say with a smile. "We're just making it official."

"Can I call you dad now?"

Billy's eyes light up as if he's just been given the best gift in the world. He sets Bryce down on the ground and lowers himself to his level.

"You don't have to do that, bud, if you don't want to. It's not what you call me that matters. I can't replace your dad and I—"

"But I want to. So? Can I?"

Billy's neck bobs up and down as he swallows the emotion down and tries to spit out his reply. "I-I would be honored."

He looks up at me in disbelief.

"Are we going to do this thing or what?" Jules asks.

"Yes. We're doing it." I laugh.

"Good, then let's go get you ready."

Jules tugs me to the concession stand where she has a makeshift salon set up. "How did you guys manage all this?" I ask.

"Money talks, honey. And when he handed me his credit card, which has no limit, by the way, he told me whatever it takes to make your dreams come true." Jules shrugs.

The stylist, Lisa, works quickly on my hair while Jules puts some fresh makeup on me. Lisa is putting the finishing touches on my hair when Jules emerges with my dress.

I gasp. "Oh my God. It's gorgeous."

The dress is stunning, worthy of a princess. Not a woman walking down a football field. My fingers dance over the satin material that flows from the plunging neckline all the way to the floor.

"This is..." Tears begin to form in my eyes.

"Stop it. Stop it right now before you ruin your makeup," Jules orders me.

"Thank you," I tell her, knowing she picked it out.

"Billy wanted to help, but I wouldn't let him. I didn't want him to see the dress—bad luck and all that. So, I tasked him with something more fun." In her hand she holds a bag. I take it from her and peek inside. "I let him pick what he wanted you to wear underneath."

"It's empty."

Jules shrugs. "Looks like you're going commando."

"They're ready," Grams says from the doorway. When I turn to face her, she smiles. "By far the most beautiful and happy bride I have ever seen." She pulls me in and hugs me tightly. "Let's go get you married."

Standing on the fifty yard line, I see my whole future before me. My son. The love of my life. Everything I ever wanted is right there in that end zone.

"Wow," he says when I finally reach him.

"You look pretty good yourself there, handsome." I lower my voice. "Nice lingerie selection."

"What can I say? I'm a simple guy with simple tastes." He leans in. "And it's so much easier to taste you when you aren't wearing anything."

The minister clears his throat. I turn to face him and burst out laughing. Standing before me is none other than the player of all players, Ethan Parks. "You're kidding me, right? You're an ordained minister?" I ask.

"Don't worry, I checked his credentials," Billy assures me.

"And a true romantic. I am going to blow your panties off with this speech," he boasts proudly.

"Talk about my wife's panties again and I'm going to end that promising baseball career of yours," Billy threatens.

Ethan smiles. "We are gathered here today to join these two people in wedded matrimony..."

I turn to look at Billy. It doesn't matter what Ethan says. All that matters is this. The unspoken connection we share. Right here, right now, we silently profess our love to each other with just a look. Our eyes make the promises we both already know we will never break. Our smiles speak of the happiness that being together brings us, even through the worst of times.

When I first met Billy, I never thought we would end up here.

Lesson learned.

Never say never.

When it comes to me and him... anything is possible.

About L.M. Reid

L.M. Reid is a reader, writer, and lover of all things romance. Just a girl from the Midwest with simple tastes and dirty thoughts. If she's not busy clicking away at her laptop with an iced coffee in hand, she can be found at home surrounded by hot wheels and the love of her husband and son.

Book Bub: http://scarlet.pub/LMBB
Facebook (Page): https://scarlet.pub/LMFB
Instagram: https://scarlet.pub/LMIG
Goodreads: https://scarlet.pub/LMGR
And don't forget to join my reader group!
L.M. Reid's Steamy Romance Readers: https://scarlet.pub/LMGroup

Also By L.M. Reid

The <u>Making the Play</u> Series

The <u>Hard to Love</u> Series

Check out all my new releases at:
www.scarletlanternpublishing.com/lmreid

CPSIA information can be obtained
at www.ICGtesting.com
Printed in the USA
BVHW031056030322
630567BV00004B/190